Cracks In My Perfect Picture

NOVEL BY TRUTH

Contents

Foreword

Some people think a perfect picture comes from the film of a camera, taking in what the holder of the camera is seeing. You can focus in and out, adjust the sight, take out light, and even block out the sunrays by a push of a button that technology has provided for you. As soon as you print out your pictures you become amazed at how beautiful it is.

Some people think a perfect picture is a painting or drawing. As the artist transforms what they are seeing in their mind, they bring it to life by using different shapes and angles, multiple colors and different degrees of shades, moving in a rhythm. Now, what was just a blank piece of paper or surface has become the artist's reality.

As for me, I agree with the people who think these could be products of a perfect picture, but within those pictures a great deal of emotions are being well hid. Look beyond that actual picture shown. What's hurting in it deep down inside? What are the feelings behind it? What is the picture scared to reveal? Can you see the struggles, the hurt, and the pain? Can you see the rips and tears, the ups and downs of that particular picture's life? These pictures want you to see ONE THING ONLY and that is the visual that you are seeing of that picture's life at that present time. My perfect picture is a puzzle. It's a puzzle because it had to put its life together one piece at a time. A puzzle hides nothing from its viewers. Every fragmented piece signifies an element of its life, and its exposes to you, all of the obstacles that it had to face and conquer, in order to be whole. The indentations in the puzzle is showing the viewer its trials and tribulations throughout life; what it has been through, what it has seen and what has become of it. The completed puzzle wants to show off, not only its past but also its future, all the while imparting its present life. Therefore, as you look at the puzzle, you'll see it's still perfect because you know its history – where it began and where it ended. You know the puzzle stayed focused and kept is faith knowing that it would conquer because the puzzle is complete.

This novel you are about to read is going to boldly show you why there are cracks in the perfect picture of my life's puzzle.

Preface

Picture: 1) A visual representation or image painted, drawn, photographed or otherwise rendered on a flat surface. 2) A vivid or realistic verbal description. 3) A person, object or scene that typifies of embodies and emotion, state of mind, or mood. 4) An image, visualization and an event of time.

As you begin to see my picture; you'll see it through the lens of a man that has lived parts of his life as a: gang banger, a drug dealer, a player, a father, a husband and eventually, a convict.

This is where my story begins…on this fateful night that I asked my ever so beautiful girlfriend Crystal, if she would become my wife.

———«◉»———

Reflecting back to the time of us being "just friends", we always spent time together as though we were dating. Finally, one night, I took Crystal by her hands and asked her when she was going to become my woman. "Damn, what took you so long? I thought you weren't ever going to ask me," Crystal smarted. We became a couple that night and we kissed for the very first time.

I first met Crystal at a car wash and from that moment, I knew it was something special about her. There was something that she had inside her, something that I felt that she was going to provide me with to let me know that life was worth living. I knew she was the one that was going to make a change in me and that she was intended solely for me. At times, I was scared of loving her, and the love that she gave to me, frightened me. I'd purposely do things to her so she that she would leave me (because I had promised her that I would never leave her and that she would have to be the one doing the leaving.) Crystal never did leave. Instead, she stood right by my side. I knew in my heart that she would be the one that I would marry and grow old with.

Trying her damnedest to get me out of the streets, Crystal was getting aggravated, but waited patiently for my turn around. Even with us falling deeply in love with one another, I couldn't leave the street life behind; shooting at enemies and enemies shooting at me. Crystal cried many tears - scared that the streets would be a certain death for me. She became pregnant and told me to promise her that I'd stop selling dope and devote all of the time that I spend in the streets to her. Looking in her eyes, I said, "I promise Panda." Panda is her nickname. However, I didn't stop selling cocaine. In fact, I didn't stop anything that I was doing in the streets. I was still in the studio, still sleeping around with other women and still hating myself. I started drinking more heavily, giving birth to the Cirrhosis disease that lives in my liver. After losing our first child, we were once again blessed with Crystal giving birth to our second child, Shelton. We were married not long after Shelton was born; however, shortly after our marriage, things started falling apart—by my own doing. I was not ready to be a husband and my eventual incarceration afflicted us both.

As I sit back and chill, observing the environment that I'm in, a couple of people are asleep while the others are watching television and playing cards. A lot of the young men that I see don't seem to be taking the time to examine themselves in order to make necessary changes. Many of the youngsters hang in cliques and the people that they run with don't give a damn about 'em. Their so-called friends or homeboys use and disrespect him every chance that they get. They're scared to walk up to a real nigga and get guidance but some of the wiser men do take the time pull the foolish youngster to the side and give him a word or two of advice. It's fucked up when a young man is scared of knowledge and wisdom and every one of these nigga's that I know of and that I ran across all claim that they're real nigga's. The meaning of real has been misused by my generation for a lone time. Many nigga's think just because they been in the streets, sold dope, fucked hoes, spent and stacked money – that they're real nigga's. Well I need to tell you motherfuckers a few things. That shit don't make you a real nigga. A real nigga is a man that stands on his own. In every situation a real nigga looks for the gain and if the gain isn't found, then the escape route he takes. A real nigga always handles his business. He knows who his enemy is and he never hesitates to put that enemy to rest. He always looks out for the ones he loves and when it comes down to his family, he is their guardian. A real nigga is the backbone of the people he rolls with and he will never steer anyone of his peoples in the wrong direction. A real nigga will speak with wisdom and remove any bullshit from his path. A real nigga learns from the mistakes that he has made and he will use his street knowledge to propel himself to a higher structuralism. A real nigga will rise in the midst of and above all obstacles. He knows that he cannot be on the bottom, because the bottom is too crowded. Therefore, the top he must sit. A real nigga knows when it's time to ride above the law. He knows exactly when it's time to take the life of someone else and where to put his money for capital gain. A real nigga understands and accepts that everything he does in life, good or bad, has a consequence behind it. And a real nigga is willing to live and die with those consequences.

Nowadays the young men that walk the streets are seeing that prison is totally different from their thought process. Some of these young men are weak in the mind and blind to the fact that they actually have friends in prison. They don't even realize that the clique that they're running with is 'bout to trick them out their own ass. See in prison, no matter what you do, you're always going to get tested. You might think that all you're going to do while you're locked up is sit on your bunk and read books, stay to yourself and not get involved in other people's shit, but when the other inmates see you doing this – their think that you're scared. They're going to figure that you're too scared to get up off of your bunk and come out of your cell. They're going to think that you're a pussy ass nigga and their going to fuck with you to see if you a real nigga or not.

There are two questions that a young man will generally ask himself about prison. The first question is, "At what age will I go to prison?" And the second is, "How long will I be in that bitch?" For these young men we must ask ourselves this question too, will they even live long enough to make it there? Many of these young men try to emulate the lifestyle of a rap artist and what they talk about in their music. If this is the case, then this means that these young men are confused about who they are never having been their own person but instead trying to be somebody else.

Many young people today call the streets home and their infatuated with the night life. They don't understand that the dark and cold alleys welcome their death. They don't understand that the dope houses are praying for them to inject the needle into their veins, put the pipe up to their lips, or snort their drug of choice up their nose. For many young people, the streets become the only place to go and many of them start using and/or selling drugs between the age of ten and thirteen. In their heart they feel like the streets are calling them. Some of them had parents who didn't give a damn about then and had no care or interest for their future. Some of their parents are on dope themselves and they've actually learned how to cook and use dope from the parent! Now I can't leave out the young people whose parents genuinely loved them and taught them the right things. It was that child who rebelled and fled from the love and protection of their parents, effectively turning their life to the streets. For the thirteen year old girl that ran away from home and discovered a life in prostitution; she now finds the displeasure of living and dying with AIDS. She goes increasingly insane because her pimp keeps sending her ass away. I feel for the dead child strewn about on the blood-spattered street with a nickel size gunshot wound in their body. Their death caused by someone playing God who decided to end their young life figuring that they didn't have a right or a reason to breathe anymore. Many of the young people are ignorant, not realizing the direction that the streets are leading them. As they see and hear the haunts of what the streets bring, they become frightened and as the fog blinds their sight they take refuge like a child that hides his/her face. They try to use their hands to shield the horrors that the streets bring. The fact of the matter is – the streets never have love for those that love it! The streets are like a mansion with many rooms. You can walk in and out of it and when you're tired, you can lie down and go to sleep. You can make love in the rooms but what you need to realize is that, although you may consider the streets your home – the streets has no roof. Therefore, when it rains – understand that you're going to get wet and in some instances, you're bound to drown.

Many young people believe in the drug dealer's lifestyle. The mentality is – the only way to make ends meet is by selling dope. Others chose to live their life as a robber, hit man, pimp or simply a con man out to make money. Whatever it is they may choose, they find all kinds of ways of hustling to achieve their goals. For some, they're 60K car will be before they reach the age of twenty. For some, they will own a house before a credit report is ever pulled on them. See the street life has its up and downs. Many men have turned into hoes and many bitches' have turned into pros. I know a lot of women that's harder than most of these men out here. They've shown me more loyalty then most men have and to the women that I'm referring to – I consider y'all real nigga's!

There's a great deal of young people that can't adhere to the Code of the Streets. And believe me, there is a code. They think that snitching on another person is cool and nowadays, you even have nigga's snitching on their own mama! For me and the nigga's I roll with, we still live by the code. We kill snitches and if we can't get the person that snitched – then we get the person closest to them. This snitching shit has to stop. It's time for the real nigga's to make examples out of these bitch-ass snitches. It's funny how the District Attorney and the detectives can get a nigga to turn state's evidence on the next person by promising them a lesser sentence by cooperating, However, in the end, they wind up getting the same time as the person that they snitched on. To the men and women who find themselves handcuffed, sitting in court waiting to hear the verdict coming from the twelve jurors that heard your case – not knowing where your fate stands – know that as you stand to listen to the Foreman's verdict – time will come to a complete and silent standstill. You may very likely find yourself struggling to take in air. Flashbacks of your life might occur and it's likely that you won't even hear the words coming from the Foreman's lips. The tears will almost certainly build up, eventually escaping down the side of your face as the judge happily informs you of the sentence that you are being ordered to serve. All the while, you're thinking that it's a bad dream, however, you find yourself on the road to prison where there are others are waiting for the chance to say, "Welcome to my house nigga!"

Asking the Question

Man, we just got through having a big argument and all the things that were said are continuously replaying in my mind. After hours of driving around, I knew that it was time for me to ask Crystal that question. The clock is ticking, it's getting late in the evening and the rain had just stopped. I rolled my window down as I drove along the road so that I could hear the sound of my tires on the wet pavement. Visualizing how I plan to propose to Crystal, I reach for the remote to my receiver and turn up the music. My fifteen-inch sub-woofers pounded out the bass from the sounds of "Sade". The mood is set, this is my rhythm and this is how a gangsta cries. As I puff on my Newport and take another sip of Cognac, I lean my seat back. Falling in my zone, I go into deep thought, thinking about all the reasons why I'm going to ask this woman this question. Why should I when I know I'm not ready? I'm still sleeping with different women, still hustling, still shooting at nigga's, you name it – I'm doing it. But at this present time, that shit didn't even matter, I'm on the verge of losing my woman, the only being on earth that gives me peace. The closer that I get to her house – the more that mind races. I'm seeing so many faces, faces of my past life…faces of my present life. I even see my own life, as if I'm not the person living in it – the life that I don't like. Finally, I pull up to Crystal's house. I see her car parked in the driveway. I settled in front of the house and glanced upward at the night sky, stalling time and stealing as many seconds as possible that are needed to prepare for what I am about to do. I picked up my cell phone and called her. On the second ring, she answered, yelling out, "What do you want?" "Hold on, who da hell you think you talking to?" I brashly responded.

"You – what do you want, Polo?" Crystal asked in exasperation.

Calmly I stated, "I came to talk to you, come outside."

"What are you doing over here? I didn't tell you to come," Crystal responded.

I gave off a smirk and yelled at her, "Girl, bring yo ass outside." After she hung up, I grabbed the ring and I got out the car to place the box on the hood, hoping that Crystal would see it as she approached my ride. Waiting, impatiently, inside the car, I soon see this beautiful woman walking down the driveway. Crystal had her hair in a ponytail, her arms were crossed and by the expression on her face, I can tell that she's pissed. The closer she gets to the car, the more that I lust for her figure – knowing that I've memorized every inch of her beautiful body. I love the way she moves her hips, the thickness of her legs and thighs and how her jet black hair with a bluish tint that falls down to her ass. And her ass "umm, umm, umm" it's just that perfect. Her Asian, White and Italian bloodline mix puts her in a class all her own. Any other woman that thinks she can or wants to compete – Crystal will knock her out of the race every single time. Crystal walked straight past the ring and came to my door. She's not saying anything to me, she's just staring and I sat there for a minute looking back at her, getting lost in her eyes.

"Step back, let me get out," I said to her. By the look on her face, I could see that it was full of hate and I knew that I pissed her off good tonight. After closing the door behind me, I noticed by her body language that she wanted me to hurry up and say whatever it is that I had to say. Grabbing the box from the hood, I turn back around to face her. I can see that her entire facial expression has completely changed. Her body is slouched and her big beautiful brown eyes are full of surprise. I take her hand into mine and notice that her breathing is getting heavier and deeper. I studied her face as I formed the words, "Crystal, will you marry me?" The few seconds that passed while she gazed at me seemed like an entire lifetime.

"Polo, you're not going to get on your knees and ask me?" Crystal surprisingly asked.

I looked down to the ground then back at her and said flatly, "Crystal, it just got through raining and as you see the ground is wet baby."

She didn't care about that and she wasn't going for it either. Crystal looked at me and said, "Polo, I'm not answering you until you get on your knees!"

"Damn," I mumbled to myself, although very excited inside. "You know I have bad knees Crystal." A big smile came upon her face. Still holding her hand, I got on my knees and matter-of-factly asked her again, "Crystal, will you marry me?" She pulled me up and blurted out a heavenly, "Yes!" I slid the ring on her finger, took her into my arms and we shared a long passionate kiss.

"I'm staying with you tonight, Polo," Crystal quickly stated as we broke away from our kiss.

"No you aint, remember you supposed to be mad at me," I cleverly said.

"Polo, I'm staying with you tonight," Crystal sternly shot back, letting me know that she wasn't playing around.

"I'm not going to let you Crystal," I said, smiling at her. I told her to go back inside and tomorrow I'll have something very special planned for her. She agreed and we kissed again. I told her that I loved her before she walked away. Turning back, she stopped and looked at me and affectionately said, "I love you too!"

Back in my car, I lit up a cigarette and took a few swigs of Hennessy. A lot had just taken place is what I kept telling myself and the more I put those words in the air…the emptier the bottle of Hennessy became, until it was all gone. I drove away from the house, speeding through the subdivision hurrying reach the main road and just as I turned the corner, my cell phone started to ring.

"Hello you just pulled off, huh?" Crystal asked.

"Yeah, you must been watching me?" I retorted.

"You been drinking too, Polo. You drunk now, am I right?" Crystal flatly uttered.

"I ain't drunk Crystal!" I said emphatically.

There was a deaf silence for a second or two before Crystal cautioned me. "Well Polo, I'm going to tell you now, you need to stop, ok."

"I hear you Panda," I replied.

"Call me when you get home baby and Polo…please be careful. Don't be driving fast. I love you." That said, Crystal was no longer upset about anything.

"I love you more," I said to Crystal. As I turned onto Delk Road, I turned up my radio, allowing my system to terrify the other drivers on the street. Relaxed, I finally allowed my ears to soak in all of the lyrics that Sade was singing.

Throwing my keys on the counter and turning off my cell phone, I walk into my kitchen – headed straight to the cabinet to grab my gallon of Hennessy. I filled my glass to rim with a mixture of the liquor, ginger ale and lemon juice. Three swallows later and I'd finished my first "high ball" and immediately began mixing another one. Walking to the living room, I placed the gallon of Hennessy on top of the coffee table and reached for my gun holster. I easily disconnected my holster from the side of my jeans and positioned my Smith and Weston .40 caliber next to the bottle. As I continued to sip, I turned my cell phone back on and immediately noticed that my message indicator light was blinking. I began scrolling through cell phone – phone book, reading name after name, trying to decide which female to call first to let them know that I had gotten engaged. During this process, a call comes through. "Hello? What are you doing?" a sexy voiced asked me. "I'm not doing nuthin'... just sitting in the dark, sipping on some liquor...who is this?" I asked in an inquisitive manner.

"Is Crystal there with you?" questioned the sexy voice. Now every woman that knows me knows about Crystal, and how in love I am with her. They all know that I will never leave Crystal but still, often they've tried to pull me away from her. They always failed in their attempts; however, that did not keep some of them from continuing to try.

"Nawl, Crystal isn't over here, who is this?" I asked again.

"Polo, it's me, Mimi." I should have known that it was her by the Genuine that was playing in the background. Genuine was Mimi's favorite musical artist.

Mimi continued with small talk before inquiring, "If no one is there with you, can I come over?"

"No I'm engaged now Mimi," I quickly responded. There were a few minutes of silence and then she hung up on me. Shaking my head, smirking, I sat back on the couch, kicked my feet up on the table and poured myself another "high ball".

Different Day, Another Dollar

The morning following my engagement, my phone woke me up due to its continuous vibrations from sitting on the coffee table. I pick it up and before I can even say hello, I hear, "Polo, what's up dog this is Mike, you working?"

"Yeah, yeah," I answered with a just waking up voice.

Mike sounded happy by response and informed me, "Well you know what I need, the usual one and a half."

"A, Mike, I got some good in, some real good, good. You're going to like it," I said.

"What's the price?" Mike asked. Yawning and speaking at the same time, I bluntly reply, "Three stacks."

"$3,000.00?" Mike inquired. "Yeah," I responded.

"What time you want to meet me at the spot?" Mike asked. Because I was just waking up, I had no idea what time it was. So I asked Mike. After learning that it was 2:30pm, I arranged the meet at 4:00pm. Slamming my head up against the pillow, reminiscing on the event last night, I laid in silence for a half an hour, and then took a hot shower. As I brushed my teeth, I looked in the mirror. However on this morning, I not only saw myself, but I could see another side of me as well. I begin to see a sort of balance in my reflection. But the longer that I stare into the mirror, that balance begins to look frustratingly uneven. I want to put an end to my old life, in order to, begin a new one with my soon-to-be wife and our soon-to-be born child. This face in the mirror is like an unwanted shadow. Everywhere that I go it haunts me and it has made me fearful of my own reflection. Trying to control my flesh, I feel weak. And in being weak, I was controlled by my flesh which only allowed the demons inside of me to run amuck. Bending down to the closet floor to open my safe, I pull out two of the six pounds of weed that I had and my triple beam scale. Taking everything to the kitchen I pulled out my drawer and grabbed some extra zip-lock bags. Placing everything on the counter, the first thing I did was check my scale to ensure that it was calibrated accurately. I took a nickel and placed it on the scale. The hand moved slowly and stopped on five grams. If you know anything about checking a scale, you know that a nickel will weigh four point nine grams or possibly even five. I place the first pound of weed on the scale and it read 437 grams – that's 11 grams off. Somebody had been going through my shit and I had a pretty good idea who it was…my cousin Bryan.

Although Bryan was my cousin, he was what a real nigga would consider a bum. See, all Bryan wants to do in life is lay up in his mother's house. He doesn't work. He damn sure doesn't hustle. He don't do shit! He's always stealing weed from either Mike or me. Mike is Bryan's brother but unlike Bryan – Mike is not just my cousin but he's also my road dog. Plenty of times, Mike had to put his hands on Bryan, but he still didn't learn. As for the moment, I'll have to get back at Bryan, in due time. Right now I have to get to this money. I make up the difference by taking eleven grams out of the second pound and adding it to the first one. I filled the zip-lock bag with the weed that I had just weighed and instantaneously, the entire room started smelling like weed. It smelled as if I'd just burnt a whole ounce! This weed was really stinky, and when I say stinky, I mean it "stank"…in a good way. The "stankier" the weed was the more money I made off of it. At 224 grams, I took the half of a pound off the scale and put both the half and the whole pound in my Tommy bag. I grabbed my loaded, .40 caliber Smith and Wesson with one bullet resting in the chamber and I stepped outside – delighted in the hot summer breeze. There were a few birds scattered about the sky and most of my neighbors appeared to be gone to work. There was a calm quiet in the air. The day seemed intended for my sole pleasure. I tossed my bag in the back seat and made my way out of my apartment complex. Turning right on Franklin Road, I saw a small-time hustlers and young adolescents walking the street. I reminisced about the days when my crew and I turned this very road into a million dollar trap. Plenty of dope cats in this part of Marietta were seeing a lot of money because of us. In 1995, due to our constant grind and the type of money that we were generating, the Channel 5 News profiled this strip of Franklin Road. However, by 1997, I'd stopped making money on Franklin and moved up to bigger and better things.

I arrived at the meet spot in the parking lot of a spaghetti warehouse a little past 4pm and parked next to Mike's ride. "Man, Polo what took you so long I was just about to call you," Mike said impatiently. Mike was your typical white man; fairly built, short cropped haircut with a shaved mustache and a beard. I pulled out the weed and handed it to him. The "stank" hit Mike instantly. He looked at me, smiled and said, "Smells good, you going to have some more later?"

"Probably not, we had to get this bullshit until the usual comes in. That's why I'm only charging you three for this shit," I informed Mike. He handed me a handful of fresh, crispy one hundred dollar bills. I didn't bother to count the money because I trusted that it was all there. "Thanks Polo, I'll call you later," Mike said as he pulled out of the parking lot. "Be careful," I said back to him. I drove out the of the parking lot and up the street to the BP gas station and copped a 40 ounce beer of Icehouse and a pack of squares – Newport's of course. On the highway heading towards

Atlanta, I realized that it was 5:00pm which meant that Crystal would be calling me soon, while she sat in downtown Atlanta traffic. Within seven minutes, I come up on the Georgia Tech/North Avenue exit. Making my way onto Peachtree Street, I encounter bumper-to-bumper traffic and on both sides of the street pedestrians crowd the sidewalks as well. I arrived at my favorite store, Bright Creation, an upscale clothing and shoe store and I am greeted by the store owner. In the reptile section of boots and shoes, I glance around; however, nothing catches my eyes in particular and less than twenty minutes later, I was walking out of the store. Just then, my cell phones rings and I answer, "Hello?"

"What's up boy where you at?" asked Mike.

"In Atlanta right now, why what's up?" I responded.

"Look, I'm going to call Ken in a few so we can re-up, 'cause I'm sold out over here," Mike said.

"Ken got the usual back yet?" I asked. "Nawl...not yet. It's the same shit we got last time. I just got off the last pound an hour ago," Mike told me. "Yeah, I just got through getting off some myself; I still have some left too, so shit, gone 'head and re-up without me this time...oh yeah Mike...last night I proposed to Crystal," I said self-assuredly.

"For real dog, you really want to do it, huh?" Mike questioned. "That's the only thing I'm seeing right now. My nigga, I feel complete and my days of being lost are gone now because I'm with her," I responded convincingly.

"I hear you dog," Mike said before he started laughing. "I guess I'll be fucking the rest of your hoes now," he joked.

"You know cuz, if they let you; they let you, have fun with 'em." And with that, we hung up. It was now 7pm and the traffic was *still* thick on the freeway and I had just noticed that Crystal hadn't called me yet. So what did I do? I called her. Ring after ring, I got no answer; therefore, I just left her a message. After maneuvering through downtown traffic, I finally arrived back home and began picking through my mail. Bill, bill, bill…every last piece of mail was a bill and the bills had to be paid. I was contemplating about watching a flick so I turned on the television. I was attempting to clear my mind of the million-plus things that was going on inside of my head. Furthermore, I was still waiting on Crystal to call me. Before I knew it, I was relaxed and i eventually fell asleep.

A Night Out of Town

I'm trying my best to kill the old man that seems to consume me in order to live my life anew. I told everyone that I had come into contact with that Crystal and I were engaged and that we would be getting married soon. Now most of my lady-friends were beginning to hate me and many of them said that there wasn't any point in me getting married if I was not going to stop sleeping around with other women. A lot of the women that I dealt with were very jealous of Crystal and they wished that they were in her place. Each of them seemed to try and figure what it was that made Crystal so special to me. They wanted so-badly to know what it was that Crystal had and that they didn't. They wondered what could have me so fucked-up in love that I had locked myself into love with her. What they didn't realize is that I grew in love with Crystal and I was with her by choice – not because I had become "locked" into anything. I wouldn't leave Crystal for anybody…for none of these other women.

———※◎※———

Crystal and I drove up to the Tennessee Aquarium in Chattanooga for the weekend. Crystal had fallen asleep, leaving me up alone while we drove north on interstate 75. She was a couple of months into her pregnancy and I can tell that our unborn child is draining her physically. Cruising up 75, a high-like feeling came over me. However, for the first time in my life, the high wasn't caused by any artificial or manufactured substance. It was a natural high. I turned and looked over at her and smiled. It was a smile of love. It was indeed a love high. She seemed so at peace as she slept while I drove. Her head was lying lightly on the pillow and she'd positioned her car seat to the perfect location, I reached across and with my hand, moving her hair that had fallen from her head, covering her face, and carefully tucked it behind her left ear. I gently rubbed her cheek and then softy kissed my fingertips before placing them placed them on her perfectly shaped lips. This gesture of love and admiration was shown without her ever knowing. But somehow, in my heart, I felt like she received it all the same. I rifle through my CD case until I find my slow mix CD by DJ Jelly and MC Assault Bedroom volume 4. I purpose tune my bass down to negative three so the vibrations from my speakers would not wake Crystal. As the music began to play, I activated my cruise control and became one with the smooth grooves that were circulating through my ride. I cracked my window and fired up a Newport. Looking at the fields of green pastures, rolled up bundles of hay, flowers and trees, I began to sense a taste of freedom from the old me and envisioned myself as a man that was already married – traveling on the open road with my wife on my side and our children in the backseat playing. I craved for what I envisioned and the way that I felt. I held onto and coveted that feeling and that vision and I promised myself that it would become my reality by any means necessary. My mind was made up – I was going to have that kind of life with Crystal.

The orange-tinged sky appeared to secretly transform; competing with the bullying of a faint, dark-bluish-grey backdrop. Separately, yet in chorus with the contentious colors of the sky, the sun struggled to maintain its presence and fell beneath the earth's surface. Just as the sun had disappeared followed the 1A/Martin Luther King Blvd/Downtown exit to Pine Street and then made a left turn. We drove another 300 or so feet and made the first right onto West 8th Street. I woke Crystal and announced, "We're here." We drove around the small city admiring the buildings to do a little sight-seeing. After riding around for a little while we, drove over the Marriott Courtyard Suite Hotel. Crystal waited in the car while I went inside to get the room. "Hi Sir, how can I help you?" said this 6' 3" red-bone, amazon woman. She wore a black blazer, white blouse, and her name tag read "Kitty".

"Yes, I would like to rent a room with a king-size bed," I replied assuredly.

"How many nights will you be staying with us?" the amazon asked.

"Two," I said.

"Will you be staying alone or will there be other guests?" Kitty inquired.

"Yes, my fiancé and myself," I said proudly.

"Congratulations!" Kitty responded.

"Thank you," I said.

"How will you pay sir?" Kitty asked. I reached in my wallet, took out my Visa and handed it to her. "Your room key Mr. Dickson and your credit card, have a pleasant stay," Kitty said in an almost presumptive manner. Walking off and returning back to the car, Crystal asked me, "What took you so long?"

"Oh, this woman in there was hitting on me," I jokingly told Crystal. In an angry tone, Crystal asked, "Who!"

"Baby, I'm just playin' chill out," I told Crystal.

"Alright Polo, you going to make me get out this car and whoop that bitch ass!" I pulled up to the valet attendant, gave him my car key, and proceeded to retrieve our bags out of the trunk of my car. Crystal and I casually walked into the lobby or the hotel, observing the amenities and taking in the sights before making our way to the elevator. As we entered our room, we noticed that the décor was very nice. There was a king-sized bed that seemed larger than it was supposed to be, extra pillows, a coffee table with two chairs, a night lamp and a 42-inch Zenith flat screen television. In the bathroom, on the towel rack were the whitest and most perfectly hung towels that I'd ever seen with the name "Marriot" embroidered into each one of them. There were even extra towels in the bathroom already. Accompanying everything else in the room was a welcome card along with a number of sweets for us to eat at our discretion. After getting settled, Crystal told me that she was hungry, so I picked up restaurant book that was on the table and looked for different locations to eat at. Finding nothing that matched her taste, we decided on pizza. I called Papa Derrick's and placed a pickup order. Occupying myself with the remote control, I turned the television to the HBO channel. Crystal was busy unpacking her beauty care products from her travel bag. After what seemed like ten minutes but in reality was more like 30 minutes, there was a knock at the door. Crystal reaches for her purse and walks over to open the door for the pizza delivery man. Although I told her that I would pay for it – she ignored my words, paying me no attention and settling the debt for the pizza. As she walked over to the bed with the pizza, I asked her, "Didn't you hear me say I got it?"

"Yeah, I heard you, and I also knew that if you paid for it, you weren't going to give him a tip," Crystal said knowingly. "I was going to tip him Crystal," I said with a presumable look on my face. "Yeah, right Polo. I have to beg you to leave tips every time we go out," Crystal shot back. After we ate, we lay in the bed holding and kissing one another and we began to talk about life. "Polo," Crystal started out as she seemed to search for the right words to say, "baby, do you want us to have a boy or a girl?"

"Girl," I said exactly. "So, you want our first child to be a girl?"

Crystal expounded. "Why? Is something wrong with that?" I asked and stated at the same time. "No, I think we are going to have a boy," Crystal told me. I reiterated to her that I wanted a daughter and explained to her that I desired a woman-child because I believed that a little girl would instantly cause a change in me and put a stop to all of my shit that I was into. Indeed, having a daughter scared the shit out of me. I felt like I would have to protect her at any and all costs. I would have to be her shield, her warrior – fighting off all evil that would certainly come her way. I'm not saying that I would not feel the same way if we had a boy; however, I am saying that I know that it would be different. With a man-child, I could, in my mind, relax a bit more. You know, let my guard down a smidgen and let him roam and discover the ways of the world.

Crystal also brought up our wedding, asking me what colors I wanted, the location and the date...among other things. I didn't really know about any of the particulars just yet but I told her that, "I want it to be big and very lovely." I leaned across the bed and we kissed. She looked into my eyes and gently said, "I'm in love with you." Staring at her while playing in her hair, I spoke back, "You know Crystal, I want to grow old and spend my entire life with you. I need you baby. I want a life full of happiness with you. Marrying you will be the best thing I've ever done in my life." A tear ran down the side of her face like a single raindrop descending on a window. Slowly, I wiped it away and as the night grew old, we fell asleep in each other's arms.

Crystal woke up early the next morning, excited about the day. Midway between her getting dressed so that we could leave, Crystal walked over to the bed and shook me awake and ordered me into the shower. I laid in the bed a little while longer before I heard her scream out, "Polo, get up! We have to get the day started!" She crawled onto the bed, laid atop my back and in a sexy voice she said to me, "Baby, I know you're not a morning person, especially when you don't have

to work, but the *two* of us are hungry. Can you please get up baby?"
I looked up at her from the corner of my left-eye. Staring, I said,
"The keys are on the table. You go eat and by the time you get back,
I promise I'll be up and ready." She jumped up, hit me in the head
with a pillow and forced my ass to get up.

Admiring all the different sea animals, the colors, and the environment in itself, Crystal and I held each other as we glared into the
aquarium glass. There were little kids around us, tapping on the glass
and yelling out "oohs" and "awws" as the fish swam by. Excited by all
the sharks, stingrays, sea horses, jellyfish and corals, Crystal and I
start feeling like kids ourselves. We spent hours walking around and
watching the fish get fed, watching the short informational films the
various species or fish, playing with the manatee's and sharks in the
"touch tank".

After returning to the hotel from our aquarium visit, Crystal
tells me that she wants to watch a porno. We scroll through the
various titles on the screen until we agree on, "N - Every Hole".
As the movie begins, there is this woman being penetrated in every
hole of her body. "Damn!" Crystal said, looking at me, "you ever did
a woman in her ass?" Looking at her with a concerned look on my
face, I answered, "Yeah, plenty of times. Why?" I asked. "Polo... you
nasty. That is disgusting."

"Nawl, baby, ain't nothing wrong with that. Women enjoy it," I
told her. "Well, I don't care. You still nasty, Polo," and she playfully
punched my stomach as she said it. I curled up because her punch
was unexpected. After watching the movie, we decided to put on a
porno of our own.

The next morning, we checked out of the hotel. We drove to
a gas station in what appeared to be the poor-side of town. Black
women and men were hanging out and I could tell this gas station
was a local trap. No sooner than I realized what it was, I began seeing drug transactions, hand-to-hand, drop offs, pick- ups and a little

bit of everything else. There were women prostituting and junkies walking up and down the street. There was a lot of traffic period... a lot going on. As I got out to pump the gas, I saw that there were many sets of eyes on us, like we did not belong here. Crystal rolled down her window and asked me something that shocked the shit out of me, "Polo, where's your gun?"

"Under my seat," I said and then asked, "why?" She didn't respond to my statement or my question. She simply rolled the window back up and sat stoic. As continued to study the happenings around me, I began to think to myself that I needed to come back up here and flood this area with my dope. As the tank was filling up, I walked into the gas station. After 4 or 5 steps, I heard the muffled sounds of thuds. I turned around to look at Crystal and she looked at me and mouthed words "hurry up". I turned back around and continued toward the inside of the gas station. Guys were giving me the "was sup" head nod and I shot it back to them. Some of them were looking at me like, "Who is this nigga and what he doing in this part of town?" A handful of the women smiled at me. I guess they like what they see I thought to myself. I paid for the gas, returned back to the car and attempted to open the driver-side car door; however to no avail. Crystal had locked the doors and at that moment I realized that the sounds that I heard walking into the inside of the gas station were actually that of my car doors locking. After seeing that it was me, she unlocked the doors and let me in the car. I noticed my pistol resting in her lap. This was the first time that she'd ever touched a gun I thought to myself. Surely the first time that she'd ever touched mine. I asked her if she was alright and she told me, "Get me out of here, NOW! And get this gun off of me." I grabbed my gun and I handed her a cherry flavored bottle of water. I pulled out of the gas station only to get lost trying to get back to interstate 24 East. We ended up in some projects and the only thing that was on my mind was that dollar sign. If I put my dope in these projects

I could make a killing, I thought to myself. After quick contemplation, I gathered my bearings and we successfully made our way out of the complex, which took us back to 8th street which put us back to I-24 East and in the direction of Atlanta. After a nice weekend away, we were headed home.

Still Having Problems

I fell up in the Blue Flame, a well-known strip club on the Westside of Atlanta off of Bankhead Highway. Over the years, I've been told that it was the first strip on this side of town. This visit isn't for pleasure. I'm here on business. I have to holla at one of my home girl named LaLa. She's a stripper from Miami that works at "The Flame" as it's often called. Inside the club, people were everywhere. There were butt-booty-ass, naked women dancing on tables and on stage, some giving lap dances, some doing anything to get a dollar out of a player. I walked up to this fine-ass woman was sitting right in the middle of the stage. With one of her hands cuffing her breast, she brought it to her mouth and sensuously licked her tongue across her nipple. "You like what you see?" she asked me. "You haven't showed me nothing' for me to like yet Ms. Sexy," I confidently said. After I spoke, she reached down and slid her two middle-fingers into her vagina and moved them about as she looked me straight in the eye. "Bust it *all* the way open baby," I instructed her and she took the thumb and index finger on each hand and spread her honey pot wide open. I pay special attention to the wetness inside of her and also on the inner part of her thighs and I say, real nigga style, "You wet than a mothafucka ain't you Ms. Sexy?" In a pleasurable, sexy and submissive voice, she said to me, "Yeah, you made me cum on myself baby." I knew it was a game. I knew that she was lying but it's all about doing what you have to do to get that almighty dollar and I respected that. I pulled my money out, peeled off a $20 dollar bill and placed it on the garter belt-like strap that she wore on her leg and said to her, "When you go back to the locker room to clean yourself up, tell LaLa to come out here."

"LaLa don't dance here no more. When was the last time you talked to her?" Ms. Sexy asked. "It's been awhile," I told her and I walked off. The sole purpose for going up there had turned into a complete waste of time. Shit, it was a waste of time and cost me $20 dollars for nothing. I'd gone to the Blue Flame to find out if LaLa was ready to talk business, so that we could make this money together. I tried calling her when I walked outside the club but her number was disconnected. I left the club and drove along Bankhead Highway, passing the Georgia Dome on Northside Drive. From there I drove past the old Hunter Homes and made my way to the West End. I caught up with some old heads that I knew at a parking lot off of Cascade Road. Out of nowhere, while chopping it up and recalling old times, we hear gun shots and bullet fragments began settling around us. Some of us dropped to the ground, while others scattered in various directions. After seven or eight shots, I could hear a car accelerating, tires screeching, as it sped away. I don't know who was in that car shooting but what I did know is that they were not shooting at me. Whoever they were and the slugs that they fired – were intended for somebody else that was standing in that parking lot with me. I jumped in my car, threw it in reversed and hauled ass out of the parking lot before the police arrived. I knew that I could have gotten hit with one of those bullets; a bullet that wasn't meant for me because I did not have any enemies in southwest Atlanta – at least I didn't think that I did. On the other hand, there was two muthafucka's that I was looking for specifically. Their names were Man and Snoop and they had robbed Mike and me in the Pittsburg Apartments right down the street from where the shooting had just taken place. On the very same night that they robbed us, Mike and I ended up shooting at a crowd of folks in the back end of those apartments.

On my way back to back to Marietta, I get a phone call from Carlita. Carlita was a pretty, little, young thing. She's Hispanic and has long curly hair – no ass though! Yet, she has a sexiness that makes up for the lack of booty. "You coming to get me?" she asked me as soon as I answered my phone. "Now what if my fiancé would have answered my phone, Carlita?" I asked.

"She didn't. You did. So, once again, are you coming to get me?" Carlita smarted. "For what," I asked angrily. "Polo," she said, just above a whisper, in a little girl voice, "I haven't seen you in a while. Come over here."

"I'll see," I told her and then promptly ended the call. I drove past the exit to go to my apartment and the next thing that I know – I'm with Carlita. Once inside my car, she began to suck my dick. She slid her lips up and down my shaft while jacking me off at the same time. She was trying her damnedest to make me cum but she still hadn't mastered the art of giving head. It took her a little while but she eventually got me off. I finished my visit with Carlita and then proceeded to drive home, knowing that I had missed several of Crystal's calls.

Later on in that same week, Mike, myself, and two of our females friends; Andrea and Sara, are eating at Applebee's, having a good time...chillin'. I finished my Sam Adams beer and went to the restroom. At the urinal, it felt as though my phone was vibrating. I reached down to see who was calling me only to realize that I didn't have my phone in the bathroom with me. This tends to happen from time to time for some reason, probably because I'm constantly receiving calls and checking my phone to make sure that I haven't missed any calls. Missed calls mean missed money in line of work. Where the hell is my phone, I thought to myself. I washed my hands, still = wondering where my phone could be and then it occurred to me – I left it on the table with Mike, Andrea and Sara. As I walked back to the table, I'm a little suspicious because I know that Sara is the type that would go through my phone, take down some numbers and call dial the numbers later just to find out who would answer. Back at the table, I checked my phone to see if anyone has been rambling through it. I was looking dead-straight at Sara and Andrea but neither of them seemed guilty of my suspicions. On top of that, I knew that Mike would not have let anybody, including those two, look through my shit. After dropping off Andrea and Sara, Mike lackadaisically blurted out, "Man Andrea is looking good. She need to stop playing and let me up in that ass."

"Go for what you know my nigga," I told Mike before he turned towards me and asked if I had a pound that I could front him until tomorrow. I went to the house, gave Mike the pound and he left to handle his business. I stayed at the house waiting on Crystal to come over so that we could begin wedding plans and our future living arrangements. I sat outside on the step and a couple of minutes later she pulled up and got out her car. She's starting to show now and I take notice. "Hey baby, why are you just sitting outside?" Crystal asked me. "Doing nothing really, I just wanted to sit here and talk to God." I said.

"Well, are you ready to go in? I got this book I want to show you," Crystal stated. She had had just bought a copy of a baby naming book and we went in the living room to go page through it. "Ok Polo, look...if we have a baby boy I want to name it after you," Crystal told me. "Hell nawl," I said in an emphatic and drawn out manner. "Why not?", Crystal asked. "I don't want our son named after me. He is his own man. He's going to have his own path and his own destiny. Plus I don't want my curses to fall down on him. I don't want him carrying on my demons," I explained to Crystal. We continued to scour the book, name after name, page after page, boy name, girl name and after hours we still hadn't come up with a name. Tired, Crystal decided to leave and head back home so she could get ready for work the next day and I decided to get some shut eye as well.

The next day was proving to be fruitful. I was out making money and I met with a couple of my clients. While out handling business, I stopped at a Quick Trip gas station to get a 32-ounce big-lid cup so that I could drink on my liquor as I rode around the city. I filled the cup with Hennessy, ginger ale, and a couple squeezes of lemon juice – a large high ball. Riding and sipping, I decide to head to Cumberland Mall to do a little shopping. Once inside the mall, I make a b-line directly to Helzburg Diamonds – a prominent jewelry store to my jewelry cleaned. On my way, I spot a woman coming down the escalator and her appearance was nothing but sheer beauty. She was in a nice business suit and her skirt had a high-cut in the back, which complimented her legs perfectly. I could tell that she had long hair because she wore it up in a wrapped style. I stepped out of the store to get a better look at her. Once at the bottom of the escalator, she obliviously began walking directly towards me. She had an even golden skin tone, around or about a size 34C-cup breast size, slightly curved hips and a round-shaped ass. "Excuse me miss, do you mind if I take up a minute of your time so that I can tell you a word?"

"No, I don't mind. In fact, I'm looking forward to what you are going to tell me," the lady replied.

"I just want to let you know that you are a very attractive and beautiful woman, and by all means, no matter what today brings, keep that lovely smile on your face. And tell that special man in your life to spoil you every day because he's very lucky to have you. And tell him to keep you waking up with a smile every day, as well," I said in the most authentic manner possible. She looked confused by the words that I had just spoken. She took two steps backwards and smiled as she appeared speechless, searching for the words to provide me a response. Before she could say a single word, I said, "I have a nice day" and walked back into Helzberg Diamonds. Never once did I look back to see if she was still standing there. I simply began putting my cleaned jewelry back on. I walked over to the Victoria Secrets to pick out a bra and panty set for Crystal. I explained to the sales associate that I was shopping for my fiancé, describe to her what type of set it is that I was looking for and gave her Crystal's bra and panty size. I ended up purchasing a lovely, sandy-brown, earth-tone colored, silk and lace laundry set. I left the mall around 2:45pm and headed home before the afternoon traffic began. Back at home, while waiting on Crystal to call, I couldn't help but have some more drinks. This time however, there was not any mix – just Hennessy straight up – no ice, no chaser. I was doing what some folks might call, "hot boxing". I drank it straight out of the bottle... room temperature. As I walked into my living room, I saw that that my phone had fallen off of the table where I left it. This could only mean one thing of course. Someone had called and the constant vibration caused my phone to fall onto the floor. The red light is blinking which indicates that I had some missed calls and/or I had messages. I flipped my phone open to discover that I had five missed calls from Crystal. Before I can dial her number, she's calling me a sixth time! "Hello?" I promptly answer. Crystal came on the phone screaming on me, "Polo, don't fucking lie to me, and you better not even pretend like you don't know what the fuck is going on. Now, tell me – who is this bitch you fucking and how in the hell did she get my number so that she could call me!"

"What?" I said to her as I scramble in mind trying to figure out what she knew and even more importantly – how the fuck she knew it. "Some bitch left me a message on my phone talking about you and how she wants to tell me something," Crystal said. "Get the fuck out of here," I said laughing, trying to defuse the situation. "Polo, who is she?" Crystal asked angrily. "How the fuck should I know!" I said. I knew that Crystal was really pissed and no sooner than I responded, she countered back, "You don't know how many bitches you're out there fucking?"

"Crystal, look, I'm not fucking nobody. I haven't been fucking nobody and you need to lower your tone and realize who you talking to," I said in a commanding voice. "Fuck you Polo. You know I'm really getting tired of your shit. Every time it's something different with you. Just the other day I went to pick Saree up from work, and when I got there, she asked me if I could take this other girl home too…" Crystal began. "So what the fuck that got to do with me?" I interrupted. "Saree asked me to show her my engagement ring after I told her that you asked me to marry you. When I said your name, this girl…" Crystal continued to say.

"Who? What girl?" I interrupted for a second time.

"The girl that Saree asked me to take home said, 'Polo? You talking about Polo?' and I told her yeah, you know my fiancé?" Crystal said, "And this look came across her face like, well it was just this look and then she tells me she don't really know you but she knows a friend that knows you."

"OK and what is this girl's name?" Dayjona or something like that," I asked, "well, I don't know the bitch and what is this message you said someone left you? You still got it?"

"Yeah, Polo," Crystal said, sounding exasperated. "Well, let me hear it," I replied. She told me to hold one and then she put the phone on speaker and began to hear the message that had been left for Crystal, "Hey, Crystal, I have something to tell you about your boyfriend, oops, I mean fiancé Polo, call me."

"There, you heard that," Crystal said loudly. "Play it one more time," I said. After listening to the message a second time, I began to laugh. "What's so funny, Polo?" Crystal asked. "Crystal, first, that message sounds like a white girl. Second, if any woman wanted to really let you know something about me then why in the hell she didn't leave you her name and her number so you could contact her? And why she didn't specifically tell you a detail about me?" I said. "I don't know Polo," Crystal replied. "Sound like to me Crystal, it's one of your friends playing games," I said. "Polo just tell me if you're sleeping around on me," Crystal pleaded. I sharply answered, "No, Panda!"

"Well, I'll call you back. I have a migraine now," Crystal told me. After we ended the call, I couldn't help but keep thinking to myself over and over, *what the hell is going on?* I started pacing back and forth, replaying the message over in my mind. I thought about all the women that I was sleeping with and which one, if any, would have actually had the nuts to call Crystal to tell her some shit like that. I also considered who had Crystal's number or access to get it? No one came to mind immediately. Mulling over the message, I couldn't help but recount how the voice on the message sounded like a white girl, so I started thinking about all the white females that I knew. A handful came to mind; however, I knew that none of them would do some foul and foolish shit like that. That's when it hit me. I thought about Sara and Andrea that day that I was there with Mike. I had left my phone on table. I sat down on the couch to really think about the possibility of either one of them doing some shit like this. I knew Sara, and if she had got Crystal's number and called her, she would have told her everything; the date, the time, the place…all the way down to what I had on! She was *that* type. Furthermore, she would have definitely left her phone and her name so that Crystal would be able to contact her. As for Andrea, well that's my play sister, so I couldn't see her doing it. She wouldn't have anything to gain. I got up, grabbed my pistol and tucked it in my pants – grabbed car keys and I rolled out. As I drove over to Sara's house, I was replaying the message over and over in my head. When I pulled up to Sara's house, I left the car running, got out and went and knocked on the door.

Sara came out and I instantly snatched her up and threw her against the door front door. "What the fuck is wrong with you?" Sara said completely shocked. "Sara, if I find out it was you, I'm going to come back and fuck you up!" I declared. "Did what Polo?" Sara asked. "You call Crystal, left her a message talking about you have something to tell her about me?" I asked, looking her straight in the eyes. With a contorted face, she replied, "What?"

"Sara, if I find out it was you..." my words ran off and I became speechless. I let her go and before I knew it, she was all up in my face talking about, "I'm not the one who called Crystal, so don't be coming over here trying to check me and shit. The one you need to be checking is Andrea!" When I heard the name Andrea fall off her lips, a look of astonishment fell over my face and I stumbled backwards towards my black Suburban. As I drove to Andrea house, everything around me seemed to be moving in slow motion. I couldn't figure out why Andrea would do something like this. Why would she hurt me? Once in front of Andrea's house, I called her on the phone and told her to come outside. She came out wearing these short shorts and a wife beater. "What's up Polo, why you looking like that?" she said. "Andrea, you called Crystal and left her a message telling her it's something she needs to know about me?" I calmly asked. "Boy, what are you talking about? I don't even got Crystal's number," Andrea said.

"Andrea, don't lie to me, not to me, we go back too many years," I cautioned.

"Polo! Baby what would be my reason to call Crystal and tell her about you? You're my brother," Andrea said matter-of-factly.

"Am I?" I asked.

"Yes, you are and I wouldn't hurt you like that," Andrea replied. "Alright then, I'll hit you up later, I got some things to handle," I said reluctantly. Andrea walked back into her house and I remembered how well she could disguise her voice. Something just didn't seem right. Back at home I waited for Crystal to call but she never did. I figured she was still pissed.

The next morning, I decided to go to work. I had not worked in about a week. That's the good thing about working for Huffy Service. You are really your own boss and you work when you want to work. As a technician, I bring home about $675 to $800 dollars a week. I ended up leaving work around 4:30pm and that had been the longest that I had ever stayed at work. I typically do not stay past 1pm. Sitting in traffic, I called Crystal, but I got no answer – just her voice mail. So I just sat there listening to her voice on her recording and loving the way she talks. When I got to my Aunt's Joy's house, she struck up a conversation with me. She asked me how I was doing and if Crystal and I knew if the baby was a boy or a girl? She also asked me if would attend church with her Sunday that upcoming Sunday. "I'll try to make it Sunday." I told my Aunt Joy. "You'll try to make it, ok. But you be in the streets all night long, doing God knows what, at least give Him some of your time. Make time for the Lord," she told me. After we got through talking, I went outside to the get my tools out of my car. While grabbing my tools my phone rang. "Hello?" I said as I answered the call. "What's up boy, you doing anything today? This Chris." Chris was one of my clients. He's a cool white boy. I like his style. "Yeah, I'm straight, what you need?" I asked. "I just need two for right now and then later on I'll hit you up for some more," Chris said. "Alright, give me about forty minutes and I'll meet you at the spot," I said to Chris. I finished getting all of my tools and brought them all inside. I took a shower and got dressed; putting on my black-cotton jogging suit that I had bought from Foot Locker and my black Jordan gym shoes.

The Holiday Season

C hristmas is right around the corner and it's a cold day in Atlanta. I'm out shopping at Cumberland Mall and I ended up bumping into an old friend of mine from high school, named Pam. Pam was a sexy ass woman I must say. Back in high school I tried my best to get with Pam, but she heard so many stories about me so she always kept her distance. I have to admit, that makes me laugh when I think about what she must have heard about me back in those days. We sat down at a table in the food court and we began catching up. We touched on a little bit of everything; especially the past and I can see that Pam has matured quite a bit from our conversation. At the end of our discussion, we exchanged numbers and right before we walked away from one another, Pam grabbed my shirt and placed her hand around the back of my neck, leaned into my face and with the softest of lips, kissed me on my cheek and then softly whispered in my ear, "Call me." As she walked away, I focused my eyes on her ass, loving the way that she was throwing that mothufucka. I must say, if a woman has a sexy walk and her looks goes along with it, it makes a nigga like me fiend about going up in it. A couple hours later and both of my hands are filled with shopping bags. As I made my way through the parking lot and to my car, I heard a woman screaming, "Help, please help!" The closer that I get, I can see that the woman is arguing with a man.

Then in an instant, he began to the beat the woman. Somehow, she avoided many of his punches and entered her car. Unfortunately, that didn't stop the man's attack and while he was trying to keep her car door open, she was simultaneously trying to close it shut. The man stopped and looked around to see if anyone was watching before his eyes settled on me. I began walking towards them and the woman yelled out, "Please sir, help me!" Right then, the man yanked open the car door and yelled forcefully, "Bitch, shut the fuck up before you get it worse when we get home!" I genuinely wanted to help the woman but I didn't know if this nigga had a gun on him or not. And if there is one thing that I know from personal experience; when you get into other people's shit, you never know what the outcome is going to be and people are often killed in these types of situations. I walked straight past them and minded my own business. Once at my car, I reached under the passenger seat, grabbed my pistol and looked back in the direction towards where the incident was taking place. I watched as the man entered the vehicle with the woman and they both pulled off together. Shit, I guess she likes being in that situation, and if she does, then that's what I call a stupid bitch. How can she expect someone to help her when she won't even help her damn self?

A couple of days had passed before I ended up going to court on an alcohol charge that my attorney worked his magic on. I walked out of court with no jail time but I did owe a high-ass fine and I was ordered to do ten hours of community service. I paid the fine the same day – before I left the courthouse but the community service… well…I'm not going to actually do it. I will just have someone write me a letter stating that I completed the required hours ordered by the court and that's exactly what I did.

Waking up on Christmas morning I looked out my window to see if any snow was on the ground but there wasn't. But you know that's how the south is and at Christmas-time, the snow is what I missed the most. If I had been back home in Fort Wayne, we would have probably had been snowed in! I was speaking with Crystal on the phone and we mutually agreed to be with one another in the next couple of hours. Around 12 o'clock, I left my house and met up with this nigga who wanted to buy three pounds of weed. After the drop, I made my way over to Crystal's house, where we exchanged gifts and then set around joking – enjoying Christmas day. The next morning Crystal woke me up at 6am to inform me that she wanted to go to the mall for the "Day After Christmas Sale". I looked at her like she was out of her fucking mind but she made me get up anyway. We arrived at the mall early in the morning. Most of our money was spent on Shelton as he is two months away from entering the world. In spite of that fact, we did manage to buy a few things for the apartment. With the love Crystal had for shopping we ended up going store-to-store and the minutes turned into hours! After a half-day at the mall, Crystal still hadn't found everything that she was looking for and I ended up spending my entire motherfucking day shopping. No sooner than the excitement of Christmas and Shelton's impending birth has passed, the New Year was upon us.

Moreover, we had to bring in the New Year the right! Crystal and I got all dressed up, looking good as hell, like we always did and we began counting down the final seconds to until we leaped into year 2000 and the 21st century. We anxiously watched the Peach drop in downtown Atlanta on television. "Happy New Year baby!" I said to my fiancé and while we held each other close, we began to kiss and tell each other our New Year's resolutions. After reciting our resolutions to one another, Crystal said that I could go out and run the streets, but only for a couple of hours because she wanted me to back at home before she went to sleep for the night. As I left the house, I called my first-cousin, Kat. We decided that I would meet her, my Uncle Bryan and my aunt down in Buckhead.

Downtown was packed; people were everywhere, all in the streets yelling, "Happy New Year!" There were people passed out drunk on the street. I heard a few gunshots off in the distance but the police weren't paying anybody in particular any attention. There were too many people in the crowd for them to point out any one person or persons. Hell, they were probably just as fucked up as we were and everybody else that was downtown. Kat asked me why Crystal hadn't come out with me. I told her that she said that she didn't feel like coming out in all that madness that was going on around us, especially being pregnant. The four of us went over to Club Carnival where the line was wrapped around the corner. I walked up to the bouncer and asked him if there was a VIP line? He let me know that there was, so I walked back over to where Kat had parked my ride. As I was doing so, a white girl ran into the back of my car with her car. Kat immediately got out of the car and started to cuss her ass out! "I'm so sorry "the white girl pleaded. I walked to the back of my car to look assess the damage. There was a scratch on my bumper; nothing major. "Do you have insurance," I asked the woman. In a timid and worried voice, the woman replied, "Please don't call the police. It's New Year's and I'm high…and no I don't have any car insurance."

"Well you know Miss Lady, right now I'm pissed, you done hit my shit," I said in my typical blunt fashion. Then Kat yelled out, "Make her ass give you some money." I could tell that the woman was high and I really didn't want to spoil her evening, so I asked her how much money she had on her. "How much do you need?" she asked. "How much you think you need to pay me for not calling the police on your ass?" I said in a serious manner. She went back to her car and grabbed her purse. She reached inside of her purse and pulled out some loose bills and began to count them. After counting, she turned to me and said, "I only have a thousand dollars. Can I give you $800 dollars and keep the other $200 so that I can have some money to party with?" I agreed to her offer, took the $800 dollars and paid for Kat, my uncle Bryan and aunt's way into the club. I spent the white girls entire $800 dollars on alcohol that night. It was a great way to bring in the New Year!

What I Just Seen

I started staying over at Crystal's a lot. So much that we used this time as trial run, to see if we could actually live together without starting World War III. I can tell you this much. I loved falling asleep with my woman and waking to her every night and day. Crystal was all I needed and in my heart, I truly knew that. That day, I need to clear my head, so I decided to drive to one of my favorite spots. Whenever I felt like the weight of the world was on my shoulders, I went the Chattahoochee River. I would sit on this big rock that is situated mid-river, between both ends. I had arrived around 9:45pm. With me, I had brought a half-gallon of Hennessy. Listening to the sound of the water I began thinking about all the dead bodies that had surely been in this river; some found and others that will never be accounted for. That's the thing that made the Chattahoochee like what some would call a grave yard and I prayed that I would never be a part of the number added as one of its victims. After a couple of hours, I was drunk and feeling good off the liquor. I peered down the river where I appeared to see three torches burning from a boat. I counted a total of five men on the boat and each one was wearing white robes and I knew in an instant that they were members of the Ku Klux Klan. I stood to my feet quickly, hopped from the rock and briskly made my way to the river bank. I broke into a light jog, headed to my car so that I could I retrieve my pistol. Upon returning to the river, I realized that the boat was now empty and that the men in the white robes were in the woods somewhere on the other side of the river. To this very day, I still have no idea what they were doing out there that evening and I really do not care to know. The next morning, I went into work and for some strange reason, my cell phone was rang ringing off the hook! Every five minutes, nigga's was calling me telling me that they wanted to re-up with they work. Seeing as though my services were in need due to popular demand, I promptly left the job around noon, went home, weighed up all the pounds of weed that I had got paid in the streets. I pulled up to this gas station, in need of gas when I happened to notice this sexy young lady pumping gas next to me and I said to her, "How you doing today sexy?" She looked up and said, "Polo, Polo Crownwel." I paused as I looked at her more closely. I remembered her face and I knew that she had a twin sister; however, for the life of me, I could not figure out which sister she was! "Was it you or your sister I was trying to holla at back in high school?" I asked. That would be me," said a voice coming from inside the car. Looking inside the car then back to the woman pumping gas, I was reassured that it was the twins that I had gone to high school with. I had not seen either of them in years. Kathy and Iesha were their names and they were both fine as hell. I told Kathy to get out of the car and when she did, I got a good look at her body and it was looking' damn good; thick with an ass so big you sit a cup on top of it. I ended up giving her my number.

And There He Was

C rystal was due to go into labor any day now and on this particular day, while we're sitting in the living room watching television. Crystal reached over, grabbed me and said in a calm yet concerned manner, "Polo my water just broke!" I jumped up, went to the bedroom and grabbed her bag containing all the necessary items needed to take to the hospital for the delivery of our child. We had prepared for this moment. I walked Crystal to the car, buckled her into the passenger seat, ran around to the other side of the car, hopped in and I took off; driving straight towards Piedmont Hospital. Her mother and step-father followed behind us. When we arrived at Piedmont Hospital the nurse rushed us inside and took us to pre-delivery suite. Crystal was having contractions every 5 or so minutes and the doctor began to monitor her. I called my aunt Joy and told her what was going on and she was excited, letting me know that she would be heading over to the hospital after she got off of work. Right there by Crystal's side every step of the way, I began to hold a plastic bowl for her after she began to vomit. Each time that she would vomit, she'd look at me with these sad little girl eyes. I wiped her mouth each time. I was excited that I was there for this blessed occasion and I was joyful that I was about to become a Father. Crystal tried me when she asked for a kiss, knowing full well that she had just vomited. I gently said to her, "Baby, I love you, but you just got through throwing up and there is no way that I am kissing you." Crystal looked at me with demanding eyes and said to me again, "Give me kiss!" Everyone in the room looked on, wondering if I was going to kiss her or not. I leaned over and kissed her on her lips, then said, "There is no way that I am putting my tongue in your mouth!" As time pressed on the birth of our child hinged on each passing second, the doctor began instructing Crystal to push and while she is busy pushing – she is also squeezing my hand so tight that she damn broke my bones. "Push baby push," I kept encouraging her. She gave out a huge push, let go of my hand and grabbed my dick instead…and squeezed it something terrible. I damn-near passed out from the pain. Now we were both in excruciating pain. Nevertheless, our son still was yet to be delivered from Crystal's womb. The doctors left the room. Within a matter of minutes, Dr. Feilgoode returned and asked if she could speak with me in private. Outside in the hallway we begin to talk when the doctor said to me, "Polo, I know that you and Crystal are not married yet, but you will be, and you are engaged to her. Therefore, I came to you first to inform you about the situation with your son. Your son is too big to be born naturally. Crystal has been in labor now for two hours, and as she pushed and pushed your son has made up in his mind that he isn't coming out so, here is what's going to happen. Crystal is going to have to have a cesarean – commonly referred to as a, C-section. A *cesarean* birth happens through an incision in the abdominal wall and uterus rather than through the vagina. That is the only option that we have for your son to be born." I looked the doctor square in her eyes and replied, "OK, let's go for it." The doctor let me know that in direct fashion that, "Having a cesarean is very dangerous. Crystal can bleed to death and many other things can happen, but I promise you that I'll be very careful with Crystal and that your son will be delivered." I went back into the room and I asked everyone to leave in order for Crystal and me to talk alone, in privacy. Once everyone had left the room; everyone except the doctor that was going to delivery Shelton, I began explaining the situation to Crystal. The doctor also explained what needed to happen to Crystal and with a signature on the consent form, Crystal agreed to have a caesarean. The nurse prepped Crystal and then relocated her to the operating room. See, having a caesarean is the equivalent of having an operation. Therefore, Shelton would not be delivered in the hospital rooms designated specifically for childbirth. We were taken instead, to the operating room where they would perform the procedure. I went out to the waiting area and told our family members what was going on. The doctor came out to the waiting area and informed me that it was time. She handed me some blue doctor scrubs and told me to put them on. As I walked into the operating room, I could see Crystal lying on the operating table. She looked at me, smiled and said, "You look just like a doctor baby." I pulled up a chair and sat next to her as the doctor began to cut open her stomach open. I was talking to Crystal while the C-section was taking place and I never stopped holding her hand during that entire time. I began playing in her hair when I noticed that she had started to cry. I wiped her tears and asked, "Why are you crying?"

"Because we are about to be a family," Crystal answered. My eyes opened wide as I saw the doctor pull Shelton from Crystal's abdomen and the first words out of my mouth were, "Man…he has some huge nuts." All of the doctors and nurses in the room busted out laughing, including Crystal. I leaned down and kissed Crystal on the lips and both watched as the doctor handed Shelton to the pediatric nurse. The doctor who had delivered then got back to the business of stitching Crystal's stomach up, leaving a small, 5-7 inch scar right below her bikini line. I told Crystal that Shelton is a big boy and joked as to how I could see why he wouldn't come out. Holding Shelton in her arms Crystal was overcome with emotions and tears began to flow down her face. I held our son for a brief period before handing him back to nurse so that they could finish their post-delivery assessment and make sure that he was healthy and everything was alright with him. Crystal told me to go home and get myself together because we had been at the hospital for quite a while. I did just that. I went home but on my way back to the hospital, I made one quick stop to make some money. When I returned to the hospital, Crystal was breast feeding Shelton. After he was done nursing, I picked him up and burped him and after a couple of minutes of rocking back and forth – he was asleep in my arms.

The Things I Need to Stop

I t was a Friday night and Atlanta was looking good. The lights from the various buildings downtown seem to bring the city to life. Crystal had gone out with one of her girlfriends so I decided to call my cousin, Mike, to see what he was up. I picked Mike up and we headed to an area in Atlanta that's referred to as Buckhead which was bustling with energy. Peachtree Street was packed, as usual, and there were people hanging out of their cars and throngs of women walking amongst the crowded streets. Mike had just popped three ecstasy pills, so he was on the passenger side rolling hard, while I was drinking on some Hennessey from my cup. Mike yells out of the window towards this fine woman in front of us, "Shawty." We made our way through Buckhead village. I was bumping Slim Coonhound's CD, "all these lonely girls want to fuck" and the music was blaring out of my system so clearly that we had women coming over to my truck and starting to dance. Right about that same time, my cell phone started ringing. I answer the call and it turns out to be Crystal, so I got out of my truck and said, "What's up baby? "Where are you?" Crystal asked, ignoring my response.

"In Buckhead with Mike, why?" I asked.

"What are you doing?" Crystal asked, ignoring my response for a second time. "Nothing, just sitting in traffic," I said to Crystal. "Polo, why are all those hoes around your truck?" she inquired. I began looking around trying to locate where Crystal was at and when I could not spot her, I asked her where was she and she replied, "Four cars behind you." I hung up and walked back to her. As soon as I reached the car that she was riding in, I said to her, "You haven't seen me doing shit, so don't start that shit with me." She looked at me and rolled her eyes and told me to go home. I walked away without saying shit. When I got back to my truck, I told Mike that Crystal was four cars behind us and he yelled out, "Oh shit!"

The next morning I got up and played with Shelton. He dug his fingernails into my lip and pulled me towards him and the shit hurt like hell. I thanked God that He had blessed me with Shelton and before I realized it, I had wafted off into a space of clarity and quiet and I prayed that my curses would not roll down upon my son. As looked into Shelton's eyes, I could see the preciousness of his life and his innocence. I knew that he had a bright future ahead of him… I could feel it. Shelton finally fell asleep so I laid him next to his mother and I sat there for a minute and watched them both sleep. Then I kissed the both of them on their forehead and left the room. By that time Crystal and Shelton had woken up, I was finishing up making breakfast. We ate breakfast, got dressed and headed over to Sear's at the mall to take a family portrait. After taking our picture, we decided to walk around to the various stores and once again, Crystal saw some shit that she liked and had just had to purchase. As she stood in line, I told her that Shelton and I would be walking around and we walked off. "Hell nawl!" Crystal said to me and then got out of line. Seeing her reaction, I stopped and said "Crystal stay in line – what the hell you doing?"

"Polo, you're not going nowhere without me, not with all these bitches in this mall. I already see it. 'Dem hoes walking up to you trying to talk and everything else. Trying to touch our son with their nasty ass hands asking you if they could hold him," Crystal ranted. "You know you're crazy as hell Crystal," I said. "Polo, you know I'm speaking the truth and that's probably why you trying to leave me here," Crystal continued. I started laughing and I told Shelton that his mother was crazy and I grabbed Crystal's hand and we all walked through the mall together – as a family.

Later on that day one, my homeboy Kale called me to let me know that he was having a cook-out at his house and that he wanted me to bring him a half-pound of weed. Kale was a small-time and I always looked out for him no matter how much he needed. Back at the house I weighed up the half-pound, and told Crystal that I would be right back. On my way to Kale's, I drank on some Hennessy. I heard the music playing as I pulled up to the house and I seen good number of women that I had slept with too. I walked out to the back porch. Everyone there was drinking and seemed to be having a good time but I noticed that wasn't anything cooking on the grill. How are you going to have a cook-out and there isn't any food on the grill? As a matter of fact, there was not any cooked food at all! I told Kale to come to the room so that I could give him the weed and after he gave me my money, I asked him where was all the meat that he was going to grill. Kale said nothing which I took to mean that he simply wasn't going to have anything to eat at his cookout. Without hesitation, I walked over to the living room, turned off the music and announced, "Hey, everybody listen up. Look there is no food in here to eat so I'm about to go to the store and get some food so if any of y'all want to eat, everybody need to give me five or ten dollars or something." Out of the fifteen to twenty people that were there, I only collected thirty fucking dollars! Before I could get out of the doorway good, Keke asked me if she could go to the store with me. I told her, "If Kale tells you that you can go, then c'mon." Keke was this red, sexy-ass bitch and she and Kale were dating but there was one major flaw about her – she wasn't worth shit. Keke got into my truck and before we could even get out of the driveway she had asked me for my CD case, pulled out a slow jam mix CD and put in the CD player. I was backing out of the driveway as the music began to play. I glanced over at Keke with a smirk on my face. Keke turned her body towards me and looked at me in a very suggestive way, then said, "So Polo, when you going to give me some of that dick?"

"You bullshitting right?" I answered. "Nawl, Dayjona told me that you was about to get married and shit you already done fucked most of the bitches in the house...so why a bitch like me can't have none? I'm tried of hearing those hoes talk about you," Keke complained. "Keke, you're Kale's woman and that's my dog," I said. "Kale is not your homeboy Polo. You barley know Kale and the only reason you do know Kale is through your cousin Bryan," Keke expounded. "You're right. Bryan is my cousin and Kale is his homeboy so that makes Kale my homeboy too!" and I ended the conversation. Keke did not take it too well. At the store I grabbed a shopping cart and Keke placed her hand on top of mine as we walked up and down the aisles. I didn't say anything to her and just didn't pay her any attention. I knew that she wasn't shit; yet, Kale had allowed her and her daughter to move into his mother's house with him. At the checkout counter, the cashier rang everything up and the total came to $387.32. I paid the bill, pushed the buggy to my truck and placed the bags in backseat. Before we could pull out of the grocery store parking lot, Keke asked me once again if we could fuck. "No," I told her for a second time. We got back to the house and I immediately started putting the meat on the grill. I had dressed it with some of my homemade sauce and Keke and Dayjona were cooking the rest of the food in the kitchen.

The following week Crystal, her mother and I, took Shelton to his doctor's appointment at the pediatric office and the nurse gave Shelton his first shot. He looked at me like 'Daddy why you let her do that to me!' and his lips started to quiver before he burst out in a shrieking cry. I felt like beating the shit out of that nurse after seeing my son cry like that but I knew that she was only doing her job and that Shelton had to get the shot to stay healthy. After arriving back at Crystal's parent's house, Crystal asked to speak to me. We went into the room where we could talk and she asked me, "I thought you promised me that you would stop selling drugs once Shelton was born."

"Do we have to talk about this shit right now Crystal?" I asked in an aggravated tone.

"Yes Polo, we do. You don't have to sell dope no more and you know that. And all this leaving the house late at night along with your cell phone ringing every five minutes, all that shit is about to stop," Crystal demands. Crystal's mother walks in on us as we were arguing and said that Shelton wanted his mommy and daddy and then she handed him to me and walked out of the room. We began to watch television and out of nowhere my cell phone started ringing. Crystal gave me a look of disgust and opened my phone and turned it off. My money ain't right for me to get out of the game right now and everyday I'm spending money on shit I can't even see. One thing I do know, a broke man can't do shit in this world if he don't have a nickel in his pocket. He can't even buy a piece of gum and I'll be damn if I'm going to be a broke ass nigga. At this point in my life I'm like a ship out at sea; getting tossed and thrown back and forth by the waves. I just can't stop. I know a slow nickel always beats a fast dime, but I love money and I always made it fast. I know these streets. I'm married to them but I also know that I'm not gone last much longer living in them either. It started raining and I walked outside. The wind was blowing so hard that it damn-near knocked me down to the ground and I could tell by the thunder and lightning that it was going to rain all night and rain hard. I went back inside to get my phone. While Crystal was asleep I checked my messages. I hopped in my truck and hit the streets to make back the money that I had missed out on earlier in the day. One of the messages I had received was from Kathy so I returned her call. "I figured you wasn't going to return my call its one o'clock in the morning so I thought you were sleep by now," Kathy said in surprising voice. "I was with my family and everything," I replied. "You're soon to be wife let you leave the house this late, she must really trust you," Kathy said. I didn't respond. There was a moment of silence and then Kathy asked me to come over. I stopped by the store to buy a pack of Newport's. My phone rang. I answered and it was Sara. She wanted me to come over to her crib and I told her that I might but I also told her not to wait up for me. I got back into my truck and proceeded over to Kathy's house. Over at Kathy's I made my way towards her bedroom, where both of her kids were asleep. We went into the living room and watched television. I was drinking on my Hennessy when Kathy's twin sister, Nichole walked in on us saying, "Oh, what's going on in here? Hello Polo." After speaking, she left the living room and for a while Kathy didn't say anything to me. It seemed as though she felt awkward knowing that I was about to get married. Two hours had passed before I told her to walk me to the door. Once outside, she asked, "So you going to call me later?"

"Yeah I'll call," I told her. I knew that she wanted to tell me something else but she held back. She grabbed my hand and started rubbing her finger on top of it in a slow and sensuous motion. "Call me Polo," Kathy said to me before walking back inside her house.

I Can't Believe What I Just Heard

After we looked at the two-bedroom apartment at Winter Set Apartments in Marietta, Crystal and I decided that this was where we wanted to live. We went to Publix and I got a $300 hundred dollar money order for the application fee. After filling out the application and submitting it, we left the office. Crystal had a huge smile on her face and she was really excited about getting our first place together. We stopped and ate at a Chinese restaurant off Howell Mill Road. While we ate, we discussed our plans. I told Crystal that I only wanted us to say in the apartment for a year and that by the time our lease was up we should have had enough money to put down a substantial down payment on a $150K-$200K home. We had not gone out much since Crystal have given birth the Shelton. That being the case, I told her that we were going to go out later that night but she said no because she did not think that she looked good. The weight gain from the pregnancy was an issue for her. I did not say a cross word because I did not want to start arguing. Still, these excuses about her weight and looks are starting to piss me the hell off. Every time I try to go out with her it's always a fucking excuse. I know some women go through these withdrawals for the first two or three months after they deliver a child but damn – I'm tired of this shit! "So what you want to do Crystal?" I asked. "Let's go to Block Buster and rent a movie and stay in for the night," she suggested. I agreed and for some strange reason, that evening felt so good. Maybe it was because I was at home with the two people that I love most. Shelton fell asleep on the first movie and when the second move was over I asked Crystal if she would clean out my ears and I placed my head on her lap. I fell asleep while she was cleaning them and she woke me by trying to squeeze a "black head" on my forehead. "Got damn Crystal! Warn me next time you about to do that shit!" I grumbled. She began to laugh and we started playing with each other. I got on top of her being very aware of the stitches in her incision from the C-section. I was playing in her hair when she touched my face and said to me, "Polo, don't leave me." I looked at her, confused. After thinking to myself for a couple of seconds, I said, "Why would I leave you Crystal? There isn't nothing in this world that I would leave you for. You're the only one for me, Panda." She reached up and pulled my face close to hers and said, "Don't ever leave me" and we began to kiss and made love throughout the night.

The next day we got a phone call from the property manager at the apartment complex and she told us that she needed both Crystal and I to come back in and see her. We arrived to bad news. The property manager informed us that in order for us to secure approval for the apartment separately, we both had to earn three times the amount of the monthly rent which was $875.00. I had been approved. Conversely, Crystal had been denied because her monthly income fell short by $100.00. She further explained that if we were married, that we could combine both of our incomes together and if we still wanted the apartment in the interim, that the only name on the lease would be mine. Crystal did not like that shit at all. The property manager told us that she would give us a couple of days to think about it before we made our decision. Now my mind was already made up but I could tell by the look on Crystal's face that this was going to be a major problem. In the car, I told Crystal that it was fine for me to get the apartment in my name and that we would still move in that week before she looked at me and announced, "No! This is going to be our first place together and I want *both* of our names on the lease, not just yours and this bitch could have approved me too…I was only off a hundred dollars!"

"Crystal we can still get the apartment; you tripping," I said, frustrated. I had hardly finished my statement before Crystal chimed back in, "No Polo, you tripping and tell me why you waiting so long to marry me?"

"Nigga…you really tripping' now!" I said emphatically. "Answer me Polo!" she demanded. It was at this point that I really started to get pissed off and with a loud voice, I responded, "Answer what? Why we're not married yet? You know the fucking answer to that shit. We haven't set a date yet!" I have no idea where she's going with this argument but what I do know for sure is that she's mad as hell about this apartment situation. "So what do you want to do Crystal, go back in there and tell the woman we don't want the apartment because your name can't be on the fucking lease?" I presented in a rhetorical manner. "No Polo. No!" Crystal said, her voice rising. "Then tell me what the fuck you want me to do!" I asked. "Marry me now Polo, let's get married now," she said. "Now…what the fuck you mean by 'now'. So now you telling me that you don't want a big ass wedding, you don't want to walk down the aisle or be in a beautiful ass dress?" I scorned. "Polo, you know I want that, but I want to get married now," she said. I looked Crystal straight in the eyes and I could see that she was drop-dead serious but I knew deep down; way deep down inside of me – I knew that I was not ready to be a husband. Now was not the right time for me to marry Crystal. My shit was not together. "Crystal, I'm not ready to get married, not yet," I mustered. Crystal looked up at me and said with this evilest voice that I'd ever hear come from her mouth, "Fuck you Polo and get the fuck out of my life!" Crystal had never spoken to me like this before and the shit that she said hurt me real bad. It left my body feeling numb and my spirit empty. Very calmly, I replied back,

"Crystal, I don't know what the fuck your problem is, but if you really want to get married now, then baby let's go down to the court house in the morning and get married." That following morning, we went to the blood testing center to have our blood taken (the state of Georgia eradicated this requirement on July 1, 2003) and the very next day we received our results. We drove straight to the Cobb County Superior Courthouse. I did not want to marry Crystal like this. I wanted our wedding to be beautiful and exciting and I wanted all of our family and friends to be there. I wanted a traditional wedding but even more importantly, I knew that I was not ready to become a husband. The judge came out and called us to her chambers. She began speaking, "We are here on this fourth day of April two thousand and one and I'm here to bring this man and woman into holy matrimony. Do you Polo take Crystal to be your lawfully wedded wife to have and to hold, through sickness and health, for better or worse, for richer or poorer till death do you part?" I was scared as hell by this point. I knew that I wasn't ready but looking at Crystal and knowing the kind of love that I have with her...I said, "I do." She had begun to cry just as I was saying I do. The judge asked Crystal the same vows as she had asked me and to those vows, Crystal replied, "I do." We slid the rings on each other's ring fingers. The judge pronounced us husband and wife and said, "You may salute your bride." We kissed and walked out of the front doors of the courthouse; husband and wife. We drove back to Crystal's house and when we got there she called her mother and told her that we'd just gotten married. Her mother was in Florida, along with Shelton, visiting Crystal's grandparents. I called up everyone that I knew and they all asked me why didn't we have the wedding like we had planned and even after I explained the reason, everyone was still happy for us. The next day Crystal and I went back to the apartments and showed the woman our marriage license and she gave us a new lease to fill out together. We were approved and both of our names appeared on the lease agreement. We had gotten our first place together.

Problems Already

I had gotten a call from Derrick, the CEO of the record label that I was signed to. He needed me to stop by the studio and when I got there we had a meeting about some future projects. He also told me that some major recording labels had inquired about signing me. Two of the major label deals have already gotten fucked up due to Bryan, Ace and Derrick's greediness. If there is one thing that I say about being greedy, it's this: Being greedy will get you nowhere! So the deals with Bad Boy and Sony Records are off the table. Ever since Derrick had messed up one of my deals, I had stopped paying him any attention. I had fulfilled the contract that I had signed with him and walked away from Head-Bobbin-Productions a free man – with no money in my pocket. I still used his studio to record my own music and I started to put my shit out my damn self. Derrick felt the tension between us and after sitting in the meeting for two hours, I can say with all honesty that it was a waste of my fucking time. On my way from the studio, I got a call from Sara and when I answered the phone she was crying. "Polo, can you come pick me up from work?" she asked. "Where yo' nigga at Sara? Ask him." I said. "He's at home." Sara informed me. "Well then you need to call him and tell his ass to pick you up and why are you crying?" I asked. "Because you hurt me," Sara replied.

"What you talking about?" I asked Sara, dumbfounded as to what she was talking about. "How could you do this to me, you're married now!" Sara exclaimed. In an excited tone I answered, "Yeah, Crystal and I went on 'head and tied the knot early, how you find out?"

"A lot of people told me, are you coming to pick me up?" I began to speak, "Look Sara I'm married now and I..." She interrupts me by yelling, "Polo, I have no way to get home, please!"

"Call a cab," I coldly stated knowing that I could not possibly be her only or last option. "Please, Polo," she begged. Breathing hard into the phone and trying to make up my mind, I said, "Look I'm coming to get you, but if you come with that bullshit, I'm going to put your ass out on the street."

"Thank you, Polo," Sara said sounding relieved. I pulled up to her job and she came out with her face all puffy from crying and shit. No sooner that she was in my car and she asked if I could take her to get something to eat at IHOP. All while she ate, I sat across from her, looking at her as she was a damn fool. The waitress came and gave her the bill and she slid it over to me. "What the fuck you giving me your bill for?" I barked. "Polo, I have no money on me," Sara explained. "Stop with the bullshit Sara. I don't know who the fuck you trying to play me for," I said unemotionally. "Nigga, all the money you make and you tripping about paying this bill," Sara jawed.

"You on some other shit. Hurry the fuck up before I leave your ass here," I warned. We left the IHOP, and then I dropped Sara off before making my way back to Crystal's house in anticipation of us moving into our first apartment together the following morning.

Crystal had gotten up and gone to work. After I woke up, Crystal's mother, Shelton and I went over to the apartment to inspect it to make sure that everything is up to par before we started moving our furniture and other household items. While I was looking around, Crystal's mother began wiping out the cabinets and drawers and then scrubbed the entire refrigerator with bleach. Crystal would be off of work at noon. I left Shelton with his grandmother and drove to U-Haul to rent a truck. I began loading things up that I had over at my old apartment before heading back to Crystal's house to load her belongings. After both of our things were on the truck, I headed back to our new apartment. We spent the better part of the night unpacking our things. Shelton had gone with Crystal's mother to stay the night so after a few hours of unpacking, I told Crystal to stop and suggested that we go out for a little while. She told me that she didn't feel like going anywhere and without thinking, I grabbed my keys and I left. I stopped at the liquor store and bought me a bottle of Hennessy, and then I drove to the park. At the park, I sat on the tailgate of my trunk and started drinking as I gazed up at the stars in the pitch-black sky. My phone started to rind and I figured that it was Crystal but when I looked down at the screen, I saw that it was my home girl, Phaedra and I answered saying, "What's up!"

"Hey, tell Crystal that I'm sorry for calling your phone so late, I just want to let you guys know that I got y'all a wedding gift and would like to know when I could bring it to you," Phaedra said. "It don't matter I'm out right now so I can come get it," I told her. "What about tomorrow, I'm about to go to bed, I have a major test to take in the morning," Phaedra said sheepishly. I told her to give me a call the following day and we ended the call. I finished drinking on my Hennessy and made my way back home. Crystal was asleep when I got home, so I went and lay next to her. Right then she woke up and asked me where I had been. "Just riding around, clearing out my head," I said.

"I'm mad at you Polo," she snapped back!

"Yeah I figured you would be," I said I already knew what she telling me.

"Our first night in the house and you decide to go out, I'm so mad at you right now," Crystal vented. "It wasn't like that Crystal, I asked you to go out with me but you didn't want to go. I been in this motherfucker all day and I wanted to get out for a second," I said giving my perspective on the issue. "Well I'm glad your home," she responded and with those words, we both fell asleep. First thing the next morning, our furniture from Rooms-To-Go was delivered. Once they had set everything up in the apartment, Crystal went over to her mother's house to pick up Shelton.

A month into our marriage and already there's chaos. My cell phone bill had come to the house and Crystal opened it. She studies the numerous calls listed on the bill. Some of these calls took place at one, two and three o'clock in the morning; therefore, I knew what we were going to argue about this shit. After going through the bill a couple of time, Crystal went in on me, "What the fuck is Sara doing calling you, along with all these other bitches? I opened up your bill and seen all the times you talked to hoes and some of the nights you were talking to them you told me that you was in the studio but you was with these bitches. You be coming home, all in the wee hours of the morning drunk and shit. Coming home at the times that I be walking out the door on my way to work. You barley spend any time with me our son."

"First of all Crystal, you be the one talking about how you don't look good, that your fat and that you don't feel like going anywhere and I be telling your ass that you look beautiful. But nawl…all you want to do is stay in the fucking house." Crystal interrupts me, "Polo, that don't have a got-damn thing to do with shit."

"Yes it do. You're my wife and if I tell you that you look beautiful then your beautiful, but your so worried about what other mutha-fuck's going to think of you I guess you still trying impress these nigga's," irritated now more than ever. "You know what Polo I want a divorce," she yelled.

"A divorce!" I shot back.

"Just leave me alone right now," Crystal said. I grabbed my keys and walked out the door. All while I was driving I thought about a bitch to go fuck but I didn't. I controlled my flesh this time. Ever since the day that we'd gotten married, I'd been faithful. I had not slept with another woman and I did not plan on starting to sleep with other women. What I had to figure out was how to be a husband. I understood that communication played an intricate role in the success of our marriage; however, communication is not one of my stronger traits because I hate explaining myself to other people. This would be something that I really had to work at in order to keep peace and happiness in my household. The following morning I had a studio session with Trillville and Don-P. They wanted me to drop a verse on one of their songs. I laid the verse but I wasn't feeling it like that. I knew that I hadn't put my all into it. See, I'm not a rapper that writes his verses to crunk music. I didn't feel bad though. Trillville and Don P can't rap anyway! The session was over pretty quickly. I dropped my verse and then left and I met Crystal at Publics. We bought a couple pounds of crab legs and had them steamed. After we ate, Crystal and I talked about the argument that we had the previous night. We each got our point across and after doing so; we went home and made love all through the night. Damn she knew how to through that pussy on me. I woke up around four a.m. and I went into Shelton's room and picked him up out of his crib and held him in my arms and then all of a sudden, opened eyes, focused on my face and smiled. Feeling good inside I began to talk to him. "Hey, did Daddy wake you up?" Shelton reached up and touched my face and then pinched my lip. I went into the kitchen and made him a bottle. I guess that he was hungry because he finished that shit within seconds. He released a huge burp and then I changed his diaper and for the next four hours we stayed up watching television and that was the best "Father and Son" connection that I had ever experienced. Stretched out on my chest, Shelton finally fell back to sleep. I placed him back in his crib and returned to bed with my wife.

The Hurt I Caused

Everything seemed to be going well now, well sort of, at least. Crystal and I hadn't had an argument in a while and I was still putting long hours at the studio but I was also beginning to spend more time at home with my family. I was finding a little bit of balance in my hectic life. Later on that night, around 1:30am my phone starts to vibrate. I played it off like I didn't notice that I had a call coming in, thinking to myself that it's some bitch that's calling me and I know that Crystal is going to ask me who it is calling me this late. "Polo wake up and answer your phone." Crystal said in a sleepy voice. I answer my phone and turned down the volume so that Crystal could not hear the person on the other end of the line. All of sudden, I hear Bryan say, "Hey nigga – wake the fuck up…we got a problem over here!"

"What problem?" I barbed back. In a calm yet panicked voice, Bryan tells me, "I'm here at Kale's house and these pussy-ass nigga's is talking about coming over here and shooting us and shit." When I heard Bryan say that, I jumped out of the bed, ended the call, got dressed and told Crystal to lift her head up so that I could reach under the pillow and grabbed my pistol. "Polo, what is going on and why in the hell is your gun under my pillow?" Crystal asked emphatically. I didn't answer her. I just grabbed my keys and headed for the door. "Polo!" Crystal yelled out, "what is going on?" I stopped at the bedroom door and replied, "I don't know baby, Bryan just called me talking about some nigga's is trying to kill him."

"Why is he calling you, why he can't call Mike or someone else?" Crystal inquired as she began to cry. "We just got married Polo. We just had our son. What if something happens to you; where is that going to leave us? You're so quick to be there for them no-good-ass nigga's, but when you need them their nowhere to be found. They don't give a fuck about you...about us...because if they did they wouldn't be asking you to risk losing your family and your freedom." I grabbed my phone off the bed, kissed Crystal on the lips and promised her that nothing was going to happen to me. Doing about 90 miles per hour on the freeway, I arrived at Kale's house in less than fifteen. I got out of my car, pistol in had and saw Bryan and Kale standing on the side of the house. I asked what was going on and Bryan started telling what had occurred. "Carlita's brother, Carlos and her boyfriend, Champ were talking about getting me over some money and shit." I started laughing then said, "Nigga, 'y'all alright. You know them scary-ass nigga's not gone do shit. I'm 'bout to go back home." Before I could hop back in my ride, Kale's phone rang and yelled into the phone, "Where the fuck you at nigga...talking all that bullshit?" I took the phone from Kale so that I could speak to Carlos personally to try and find out what the hell was going on. "Hello Carlos...is this Carlos?" I spoke into the phone.

"Yeah, pussy nigga this Carlos," he said full of bravado. I knew that I know who he was talking to but I kept my cool, calmly stating, "Carlos, first of all realize who the fuck you talking to!"

"Who the fuck is this?" Carlos shouted.

"Polo!" I responded almost before Carlos finishes his question.

"Polo? Bryan cousin?" he asked, sounding surprised.

"Yeah!" I replied forcefully.

"Polo, you don't got shit to do with this shit here, but if you want to involve yourself, I'll shoot your ass too," Carlos boasted.

"Carlos now you know you ain't gone shoot nobody so yo' bitch-ass need to calm the fuck down before I come to yo' house and slap the piss outta you," I informed him. "Fuck you!" Carlos shouted through the phone. "I tell you what, I just made myself involved in this shit, so you and the hoe ass nigga you wit know where to find me," I said in true G-fashion. Carlos screamed out, "WE COMING!" right before he hung up the phone. We waited and waited to see if these nigga's was gone show. Two hours had passed and still no sign of Carlos or his anybody from his camp. I decided to bounce and told Bryan and Kale that I was heading downtown. They asked if they could roll with me and the three of us rode out. It was a Thursday night and the spot that's jumping is the Shark Bar. Just as I made my way through the bar, my phone rang, I answered and it was Carlos asking, "Where you nigga's at? We here!" I couldn't believe that this nigga had called my phone but I let him know in no uncertain terms, "Nigga I'm in the city 'bout to get with these hoes out here. I don't have time for you nigga. So whatever you got going on with my cousin y'all go head up with each other."

"Polo, I'm going to show you that this shit ant no game…where the fuck you at right now?" Carlos snapped.

"We at the Shark Bar. What, you want to meet me somewhere?" I asked Carlos.

"Yeah, meet me at the J.R. Crickets in Atlanta on North Ave. and Spring Street." Carlos said.

I knew that this was some childish shit but it was entertaining to me, so we made our way down to Spring Street and North Ave. I parked and walked into the Crickets and placed a ten-piece wing order with fries. A couple minutes later, my phone rang. It was Carlos and I could see that they were parked across the street. I told Bryan and Kale that Carlos and whoever he was with had arrived and I told Carlos to follow us to an isolated area so that we could handle whatever it was that needed to be handled. I jumped

back in my Suburban and headed towards down North Ave., towards the Georgia Tech parking lot. Kale told me to roll down the
back window so he could shoot at Carlos's front windshield and
everybody in the car could get hit. I didn't want to kill these nigga's;
their lives weren't' worth taking. Besides, as I looked in my side mirror, I saw that there were four cars directly behind Carlos. Kale not
only ran the risk of accidently shooting innocent bystanders but if
he shot up Carlos's car there would possibly be any number of eye-
witnesses to a murder. I told Kale, "No" but as soon as I said it, the
white Crown Victoria that Carlos was driving got in the right lane
and accelerated. Once the car reached my back-right bumper on the
passenger-side; they opened fire. I was in high-pursuit now. Carlos's
car was about a foot ahead of me trying to get away and we started
shooting back. Both cars were traveling at a high rates of speeds and
in the distance, I could see that we were fast-approaching a police
cruiser. The closer that we got, I realized that the cruiser was sitting
the Georgia Tech parking lot and as we passed him, I just knew that
he was coming after us. Carlos's Crown Victoria was faster than my
truck and they got away from me, which made me especially pissed.
In addition to being pissed – I was also amazed because I would
have never thought that these pussy-ass nigga's would have had the
heart to shoot at any nigga. Carlos and whoever he had riding with
him no killers though. Cause if they were, they would have waited
for the proper opportunity to kill us instead of just shooting up the
left-side of my truck. Carlos knows that he fucked up and as soon as
I see anyone he's associated with, even his sister, Carlita – I'm going
to put a whole in the mothafucka. I dropped Bryan and Kale back
at Kale's house and as I drove home, I started thinking about what
Crystal was going to say once she saw my truck. I knew I would not
be able to explain my way out of this one and when I got home, I
got straight in the bed and lay down beside my wife. In complete
silence, I watched her as she slept. Looking at Crystal, I realized just

how much I loved her and I knew that I would die for her. My conscience was getting the best of me now I and I began cussing myself out about the stupid shit that I was out in the streets doing when I knew damn-well that what I have at home makes me a better man and is better than anything out in the streets. I fell asleep conflicted.

A couple of hours later Crystal had turned off the alarm clock, got up and took a shower to get ready to work. While in bed, I heard Crystal's mother walk through the door. She and Crystal spoke for several minutes before they left the house leaving me alone. Around two o'clock I got an anonymous phone call. I answered my phone and said, "Hello!"

"Yeah, can I speak to Polo?" an unknown voice asked.

"This is me, who is this?" I inquired.

"Polo, look you don't know me but I was in the car last night wit Carlos and Champ…"

"Oh, you muthafuck's are dead!" I said cutting him off.

"See that's why I'm calling you. Champ and Carlos came by my way talking 'bout your cousin. Bryan had stolen some shit from them and they were going over there to get their shit back and they wanted me to come along. Last night, after the shootout, when we got back to the crib, I found out the real reason behind the situation. It wasn't about no shit being stolen at all…it was over some pussy," the caller said.

"Over a bitch, huh!" I said to him. "Champ is mad because Bryan is fucking his girl Carlita and last night before all that shit went down Carlita and Champ was fighting and she told him that she had just fucked Bryan a couple of hours ago. Carlos, Carlita's brother, is mad at Bryan because the girl that Carlos is seeing wants to fuck Bryan too and he found out that they were supposed to get together last night," the voice on the other end of the phone explained. "It sounds like a bunch of bullshit to me player," I responded. "Polo, I'm just trying to tell you what's going on and that if I knew that it was over some pussy, I wouldn't have got involved. I also wanted to tell you that if you want to know where Champ and Carlos are right now; then I'll meet up with and show you and we can both dump on them nigga's," the man said. I told oh' boy thanks and let him know that I would get up with him and I hung up the phone. I know that this is a bunch of bullshit. First of all, how did this nigga get my number and secondly, this shit is probably a set up. I stepped outside with a glass of Hennessey and I lit up a Newport and started talking to God. I asked God to open my eyes and allow me to see the blessings that He had afforded me. Looking to the sky, I saw a blue jay fly across my visual path and landed on the tree next to me and started chirping. I went back into the house and poured myself another drink.

Later that afternoon, Crystal came home with Shelton in tow. That's when all hell broke loose! "Polo, why are there bullet holes in your truck?" Crystal yelled at me. "Baby don't worry about it," was the only words that I could muster.

"What the hell you mean...don't worry about it! I knew that was going to happen, that's why I begged you not to go," she demanded.

"Crystal, I don't want to hear this shit right now," I said.

"Well you're going to hear it," and as she rambled on, I blocked out what she was saying, grabbed my keys and my gun and walked out of the house. By now, my mind was racing in every direction, flashbacks are popping in and out of my head and I found myself thinking back to all the shit that I'd been involved in from a child all the way up until present time: the shootout from last night, all the women that I had fucked, Crystal and me, Shelton's birth. I thought deeply about all the time that I had spent locked up and the times that I had been laid up in some hospital with blood all over my body. Two days later, Crystal found a picture and a phone number from another female and the arguing started all over again. For a second time, she told me that she wanted a divorce. I walked out as soon as the statement left her lips and drove over to Mike's house to kick for a few hours. I told him to ride back to my house with me but when we got there, the entire apartment was empty. "What the fuck is going on," I said out loud, my words echoed off the bare walls. I looked at the empty living room, the empty dining and the empty kitchen. The bedrooms were also empty, as were the bathrooms. The only thing that she left was the nails in the wall that we'd used as an anchor to hang our picture. I called Crystal but she didn't answer the phone. Next, I called my cousin Kat and she told me that she was on the way over. I was on the phone with my mother as I opened up the refrigerator and saw that there was nothing inside of it! As I closed the refrigerator, I saw Crystal walk through the front door and the first thing out of my mouth was, "Bitch, where the fuck is my shit?" My mother yelled out on the phone, "Polo, don't you hit that that girl, I'm on my way over!" Crystal stop dead in her tracks and questioned me with a baffled look on her face, "Bitch… so now you're calling me a bitch?" She walked through the room as I stood in the doorway. A few seconds later, Crystal's father walked up and asked if he could speak with me. "Polo, I don't know what is going on but Crystal told us that you been sleeping with other women and you know as well as I do you that can't be doing that now that you are married. Crystal had also said that she was moving out and that's why I'm here. Give her some time with this Polo and the two of you come back together and work it out." After talking to Crystal's father – and uneasiness came over me so I walked outside only to discover the rest of Crystal's family. The closer that I got them; the clearer I could see their faces. I wanted to tell them that I was sorry but the words never formed from my mouth. My mother and Kat pulled up and the situation instantly got worse. Kat asked where was Shelton and Crystal's mother spoke out, "I don't think Shelton needs to be around his father." Kat looked at Crystal's mother like she was straight-crazy and asked, "So what are you saying, we can't see him, you ant his mother."

"No Kat I'm not but I am his grandmother and I think that

neither Shelton nor Crystal need to be around Polo right now. He has people shooting at him. Have you seen his truck? There are bullet-holes along the passenger side. What if that would have happened when Crystal and Shelton was in the truck? I don't think none of us need to be around him…he has people trying to kill him!" Kat and Crystal's mother began going back and forth and it got so heated that Kat walked up on Crystal's mother and was about to hit her. I caught Kat's arm and pulled her towards me. I wrapped my arm around her neck and walked her down the street. There was increasing tension and confusion on both sides of our families and as I looked around I knew that this entire situation was my fault. Crystal walked up to me and held my hand. We stared at one another without blinking and then she walked away, got into her mother's car and pulled off…never uttering another word.

Still Up to No Good

I have not talked to my wife or seen my son for an entire week now and really want to see them badly. I never called Crystal after she left our apartment and I had just been waiting time out and hoping that she would call me soon. It was a Friday night and Mike and I had gone out to a club on Bankhead Highway called Atlanta Live. Some people call it "The Bounce". The Bounce is a club where most of the drug dealers around the city go, the atmosphere is always crunk. College women and local ladies dance on the floor while nigga's be ballin' in VIP. The rest of the patrons stay posted up on the walls. Popping pills, smoking weed, drinking or snorting cocaine is how most of the people party up in The Bounce. It's not just inside the club either because outside the club, music blasts from idle cars in the street locked in bumper-to-bumper traffic. You can always find a club outside of a club in Atlanta. Inside the club Mike and I made our way to the bar and we'd usually spend five to six hundred dollars on liquor. In spite of this fact, being that it was only he and I and we weren't in the mood to kick it like that tonight – we settle on spending five or ten dollars at a time. We walked around the club and I began to see folks that I hadn't seen in a long while, females that I hadn't seen in years and nigga's that I had beef with back in the day. The time that we spent in the club was cool but it didn't take my mind off of the problems that I had going on at home. Mike looked over at me and I think that he could see the stress on my face and he asked me, "Polo, you ready to go?"

"Yeah, we been here about an hour let's go," I told Mike.

"Yo', Keke and Ice wants us to come by the GC and kick it with them for a minute," Mike said. "Nigga, I don't care what we do," I responded. We drove over to the Gentlemen's Club (often referred to as the "GC") and when we got there the smell of pussy way all in the air. The GC was a strip club in Atlanta and a lot of celebrities and hustlers can be found there on any given night, chilling. This Friday night was no different. Watching the naked women dancing on the stage, I walked around and thought about which female in my phonebook that I was going to call and go fuck after we left the strip club. We sat down at a table as Keke gave both of us a hug and asked us if we wanted anything to drink. "Polo, I already know what you want to drink, Hennessy straight; you ain't nuthing but an alcoholic!" I started laughing and I asked Keke where Ice was at and she pointed her finger in the air in no direction in particular. I decided that I would just walk around and find her. Keke gave Mike a kiss while she reached down and grabbed his dick. He yelled out, "Stop!" and then she walked away. "Mike, I thought you weren't fucking with Keke any more…by what I just seen nigga you still going up in that pussy," I joked. Mike didn't say anything, he just laughed and within a couple of seconds, Keke came back with our drinks and then she left again. I was on my fifth shot when Ice walked up to me in a blue, G-string with matching high heels. There was glitter on her face and I can honestly say that she looked real good. Ice sat down next to me and said above the music that was playing, "I haven't seen you in a while." She looked down at my hand and noticed my wedding ring. I responded to her comment before she interrupted me with a compliment, "Nice ring, I heard that you went and got married on me. Tell your wife that she is a very lucky lady." I looked at her with a smirk on my face and that's when she looked down at my pants and spread her legs wide open which allowed me to see her pussy-print. She looked back up and I told her, "I'm having problems in my marriage. I'm taking my wife through a whole lot of shit."

"If your wife was smart then she'll stay by your side and see past your shit…I would." Ice got up but before she walked away, she sarcastically asked, "You ain't been giving none of these tramp-ass hoes no money right?"

"Naw baby I don't give out money that easy," I replied.

"You better not…I'll be right back."

The ensuing night, I was on the phone speaking with Maria; a shapely, petite Dominican with long, black curly hair. "What you doing Papi?" Maria asked in a sultry voice. "Nothing, laying here in the bed wishing you was here," I said in a relaxed tone. "Oh, you do huh, but I told you Papi, I have a boyfriend," Maria reiterated. "So you're going to let him stop you from doing what you want to do?" I countered. "Polo stop baby, change the subject please. Are we still going out?" Maria asked. I got up off the bed and went and picked Maria up from her house and we went to dinner. After dinner, we took in a movie and then I dropped her off back home and the proceeded on to my house. Crystal called me while I was on my way home and said that Shelton wanted to see me. I let her know that I was on my way and she told me that she was already there. I was having a great time, playing with Shelton. I asked Crystal when she planned on coming back home and she said, "I don't know Polo, I need time to think and it's too much for me right now…way too much." I looked at my wife and ran my fingers through her long, silky black hair. "Baby I miss you. I need you and our son to be here with me and I'll work on me Crystal. I promise. I'll never hurt you again, just come home," I appealed to Crystal. "In time Polo, but know I still love you and I miss you as well," she reassured me and then she took me into the bedroom and we made love.

A couple of days later I went out with this girl name Misty and one of her girlfriends. I had met Misty one day after leaving the house after one of me and Crystal's big arguments and I had promised myself that I was going to talk to the first girl that I saw and that ended up being Misty. I took them to the bowling alley and we kicked it for a while before I dropped them back off and headed back home my own self. As soon as I made it home, I went straight to the kitchen and poured myself a drink. Sometime around 2am, my phone rang. It was Maria and she was crying. Consoling Maria, I asked what was wrong. She told me that she and her boyfriend had gotten into a big argument and she wanted to know if she could come over. Thirty minutes later she was at my front door. I let her in and instinctively, we headed to my bedroom and began kissing and I took off her clothes. I laid her down, gently and spread her legs using my tongue as the guiding force to do so. Maria was panting lightly in pleasure. I licked her pussy in measured manner, up and down, and drew her clitoris in my mouth like a newborn nursing. Her entire body tightened in a slow and deliberate grind-like motion. She grabbed my shoulders and said in heavy breath, "Papi, Papi...I'm coming!" The sweet taste of her honey-pot; soaked from her orgasm affirmed her state of satisfaction. With her index finger, she pointed and motioned for me to move up closer to her. I took my shirt off and granted her request, then rolled over on my back. Maria stared straight into my eyes as she unbuckled my belt, unzipped my jeans and pulled them off of me. With a firm hand, she grabbed my dick throw the flap of my boxers before taking those off too. Slowly, she began to suck my dick – up and down. Her mouth was hot like the heat from a bonfire; wet with calculated moisture. The head was extraordinary. She slid my dick inside of her as she straddled me, reverse-cowgirl style. Breathing heavily, she rode my dick in a most familiar manner – like we had been making love for years. I held her hips and moaned aloud as I gazed at her luscious body. We fucked for forty-five minutes before she took my wet-dick out of her pussy and placed it in her hot-mouth. Maria took my entire nut and swallowed it and for the rest of the night we laid together sleep in one another arms.

A Stormy Night

Thundering and lighting outside with the rain coming down hard I laid on the bed talking on the phone with Misty and she had asked me if it was alright if she came over. Mike was at the apartment with me but I knew that that was not an issue. Not long after we ended our call, Misty arrived at my apartment. She and I went to the bedroom where we chilled on the bed and talked. Misty was telling me how much she hated her job. Suddenly, we were interrupted by a knock at the door. I got up and walked to the front door. As I did so, the knocking continued and I began to hear a mumbled voice accompanied with the knocks. "Who the fuck is that beating on the door," I whispered to Mike, shocked because neither of us was expecting company. I peered through the peep hole. "Polo, open the door now!" Crystal demanded.

"Oh, shit Mike! It's my wife! Go and turn off all the lights so it seems like we aren't here," I said. Contemplating my next move, I walked back to my room and Misty asked me who was knocking at the door. I told her that it was my wife. She jumped up and said that she was leaving but I made her sit back down. Looking at the patio door that connects to my room, I could see Crystal's shadow beating on the sliding glass door. "Polo, open up the damn door. I know you're here…your fucking car is parked out front," Crystal yelled as she walked back around to the front door and started knocking again as if she were trying to beat the door down. I kept saying to myself, "What the hell is my wife doing over here in the rain beating on the motherfucking door. And how did she know I had a woman over here? How in the hell am I'm going to get out of this?" I figured that eventually, Crystal would just leave and after about twenty minutes, the knocking and the yelling stopped. I told Misty that she could go ahead and leave. As she walked out, I tried to close door but before I could, Crystal jammed her foot between the doorstop and the inside of the house. "Who is this bitch?" Crystal questioned. I instructed Misty to keep walking before I yoked Crystal up. "What the fuck is wrong with you Crystal!" I grumbled. "Polo, who the fuck was that bitch?" Crystal responded. "I don't know that hoe Crystal… that bitch was over here with Mike," I said. Mike chimed in, "Yeah, she was over here with me Crystal."

"Mike shut the fuck up! That bitch wasn't here with you and if she was then why you didn't open the door when I was knocking?" Crystal barked. "I was scared to, shit! You was trying to beat the damn door down," Mike told Crystal.

"That's some bullshit and I know that bitch was here with you Polo and why you didn't answer the door?" Crystal replied. "I didn't hear the door. I just woke up and came to the kitchen and Mike told me that someone was beating on the door and the bitch that he was with was leaving so I let her out. Shit…I been drinking all night," I said. "You're fucking lying Polo," Crystal told me as she went outside and walked towards her car. I followed her and we began to argue in the rain. The lies that I told her were destroying the both of us. I felt bad because Crystal had a look of humiliation on her face and I knew that I'd hurt her, yet again. I told her to come back inside and she agreed. We got undressed, Crystal put on my blue shorts and a white wife beater and we lay across the bed and talked.

More Problems

Crystal had been talking to Misty without my knowledge. Looking back on it, I should have known because she had repeatedly asked me who Misty was. My response was always the same, "She's probably a female singer that I'd met and gave my number too." I had recently cut all ties with Misty. First of all, her pussy wasn't good. Secondly, the bitch did not know how to suck dick. Shortly prior to cutting Misty off, she had called me, talking about she's pregnant and that the baby was mine. "Bullshit," I exclaimed to her and then disconnected from the call. She called right back but I did not answer my phone. She left a message saying, "I don't want the baby. I want to have an abortion and I want you pay for it." Now this bitch must really think that she's slick because I knew that I was not the only nigga fucking her and would be damned if I was going to pay for any got-damn thing! A couple of days later, Crystal called and asked me to meet her at a payphone that she was parked next to. When I arrived, she once again asked me about Misty. "Crystal I'm getting tried of this shit. I already told you that I don't know," I reiterated to her.

"Have you fucked Misty?" Crystal pestered me. "Didn't I just tell you that I don't even know the bitch?" I replied, my voice rising from frustration. I was getting by this point and Crystal knew that I was aggravated but she continued to press the issue and said, "I got her number out of your phone when you were in the shower. She called you and I wrote the number down. I've I talked to her three times already and I know that she was the one over your house that night it was raining…now tell me the truth," Crystal demanded. As far as I was concerned, the conversation was a waste of time. "I don't know the bitch," I responded again.

The next morning I was at the studio. Crystal called and told me come home. She said that she needed to tell me something very important. As I drove up to the apartment, I saw that Crystal was sitting idle in her jeep. I parked my car, got out and walked over to Crystal. "What's wrong?" I asked. "Polo, I need to find out the truth. Misty told me that she was pregnant by you so I told her to meet us over here," Crystal explained to me. I was at a lost for words and I began scrambling for things to say. However, before I could, Misty pulled up. Crystal got of her jeep and walked over the Misty. I'm going to kill this bitch, I thought to myself. She brought this shit to my house and now my wife knows. I couldn't believe that I the two of them was actually talking to one another. "Polo come here," Crystal said and motioned for me to walk towards them. I noticed that Misty had bought two of her girlfriends with her and they were standing outside of her car as well. Misty turns her attention to me and said, "Polo you know you had fucked me, so I don't know why you're lying. All I want is for you to pay for the abortion and I'll get out of you and your wife life," she said in a condescending tone. "Bitch, I ain't ever fucked you and you done fucked up by bringing your ass over here!" I snapped at Misty. I was livid at this point and started cussing Misty out. She walked up and got in my face, woofing about this and that and then she took her right index finger and poked me in my forehead. Before she could take her finger off of my face, I slapped her. I smacked the bitch so hard she fell to the ground. Both of her girlfriends ran up on me talking shit and I began snapping on them too. They wised up got their asses in Misty's car. Crystal got in my

face. "Polo, why did you hit that girl? "Get the hell in the house…
now!" Crystal yelled at me. She walked me into the house and told
me that I needed to apologize to Misty. "Polo, does she know that
you're on probation for those weapons charges? I know she's going
to call the police. Please call her and say that you're sorry," Crystal
pleaded with me. "Crystal fuck that bitch!" I responded. Crystal was
scared and she grabbed her phone, dialed Misty's number and then
handed me the phone. The phone rang three times before a female
voice answered, "Hello!"

"Let me speak to Misty," I demanded. "Who is this?" the female
voice inquired. "Polo," I announced. "Oh, nigga we gone fuck you
up!" the voice informed me. "Bitch put her ass on the phone," I said,
looking at Crystal while I waited for Misty to get on the phone.
"Yeah Polo," Misty said when she got on the phone.

"Hey look, I'm sorry for hitting you," I said half-heartedly.

"Too late I'm going to the police," Misty threatened.

"You goin' to the police, where to Cobb County?" I asked.

"Yes," Misty affirmed. "Well tell those muthafuck's that they
don't have to come to my house, I'll come to them," and I disconnected the call. Crystal asked me what was going on and I told her
and that I was going to the police station instead of having them
come over the house. I knew I had plenty of dope, money and guns
in the house and I would rather deal with the charge for slapping the
shit out of Misty's bitch-ass than dealing with a dope and pistol case.
Crystal said that she was coming with me. "No. Just wait here and if
I get locked up, take some money from out of the safe in house and
come bail me out," I told her.

As I walked through the doors of the Cobb County Police department, I looked around for Misty but I did not see her. I casually walked up to the window and asked the female officer behind
the window if anyone had come in and filled out a report for an
arrest warrant. The officer said, "No," and then she asked me what

my first and last name was. Without giving her my name, I said, "Thank you," and then walked out of the front door. No sooner than I stepped outside, my phone rang. I heard a familiar voice when I answered the call, "Polo, this is Magail." I figured that he was calling me to buy some weed so I told him that I was busy and that I would need for him to call me back. "Hold up Polo, what happened earlier in the parking lot?" Magail asked before I could hang up. "Why? You must have been outside to know about that," I questioned Magail "Misty and two of her friends just left from over here talking 'bout she'll pay me if I fuck you up for her. She doesn't know that we know each other," Magail told me.

"Fa real…well thanks for the information," I said to Magail.

"That's not all Polo. When she left, she said that she was gone ask some more nigga's too," Magail informed me. With that, I hung up and made my home. Once there, I told Crystal that Misty was going around offering money to have me fucked up. I called Misty, "Hello Misty."

"What do you want Polo?" she asked in an irritated tone.

"Be careful of who you talk to! You don't know who knows me out here in these streets," then I hung up on her. I went into the kitchen and poured a glass of Hennessy. My wife walked up behind me, wrapped her arms around my chest and asked me if she could spend the night and maybe go and get breakfast in the morning. The following morning Crystal got up first then woke me. We left and headed out to breakfast but ended up stopping at an office building. "Crystal, where the hell we at?" I asked. "I just need to take care of something before we eat, come inside with me," Crystal answered. We walked into a waiting room where a bunch of women were sitting. There were a few men scattered about too. I saw Misty sitting in the corner. She looked up at me and I saw that her face was a black-purple in the area where I had slapped her. A woman dressed like a nurse came out into the waiting room and asked if she could help us. Crystal informed the nurse-dressed woman that we were there to pay for Misty's abortion. I looked at Crystal like she was crazy as we walked over to the payment room and Crystal paid wrote a check for Misty's procedure. I was pissed as we walked back towards the car. "Why did you pay for that shit Crystal," I asked. "I paid it because you're my husband and this girl is saying that you got her pregnant. So I'm doing what a wife would do not even knowing the truth," she replied. I told her to take me back home but before getting out of the car, I gave Crystal the money for the check that she had just written.

The Lick

My home girl Tiffany called me one day and she began telling me about I lick that I could pull. She explained to me that she saw some nigga's weighing up two keys of cocaine and that they were counting out a hell of a lot of money. I told Tiffany that I didn't fuck with cocaine anymore...since like 1998. Furthermore, I explained to her that if I ever got convicted on another cocaine charge, I would be facing a life sentence. She said that she understood but she kept going on and on about how easy the lick was. I told her that I would think about it and that I would get back with her and when I had made a decision. My girl Tiffany was an Italian woman that I had known for some years. She used to cop weed and cocaine from me back in the day and she always worked as an escort. I thought about the robbery and I even went to go look at the apartments where she had told me that the dope and money was located at. After looking the place over, I left and made a couple drops, made some money and then headed back over to Crystal's parents house to see Shelton and Crystal. I mentioned the lick to Crystal and of course, she told me not to do it. She questioned me as to why I was going back to my old lifestyle. It was an easy lick I told her. Crystal looked at me and then rolled her eyes, frustrated. The next day I should have been in Kentucky, dropping off some pounds of weed to some of my clients but I decided not to go. Instead, I called Tiffany and told her that I would pull the lick. I drove over to her place and picked her up. We drove over towards the apartment but I stopped and parked my truck in a shopping center parking lot, behind the apartments where the lick was to take place. Tiffany and I walked through the woods that separated the parking lot where my truck was located and the back of the apartments. While we were walking, I instructed Tiffany to go to the apartment unit and find out exactly how many people were inside, then to come back and tell me. As soon as she walked off, I began thinking that there was a little voice in my head telling me not to go through with it. A couple of minutes later, Tiffany came back and told me that there was only one man in the apartment. This is gone be a sweet lick I thought to myself. "Go back in there and give that nigga some pussy. Make sure that you leave the door unlocked so that I don't have to kick it in," I told her. Tiffany walked off for a second time, headed to the apartment to do what I'd told her to do. Standing there, in the woods, alone, my conscience kept telling me, "don't do it, don't do it" and up until this point, I had always listened to my conscience. Once inside, Tiffany called me and let me know that the door was unlocked. I gathered myself and then I started walking toward the apartment. Just like Tiffany had said, the door was unlocked. I made my way inside and as they walked in I could hear Tiffany fucking the shit out of this nigga. I proceeded straight to the bedroom where Tiffany had told me that the dope and money was supposed to be at. I searched the room from top-to-bottom but I didn't find shit. I walked into the kitchen and searched from top-to-bottom. Again, I didn't find anything! The only room that I had not looked in was the bedroom that faced the front door where Tiffany and the man were fucking. Now more than ever, my conscience was telling me to get the fuck out of the apartment and *this time* I had all intentions of listening to my conscience! I started to walk towards the front door to leave the apartment when all of a sudden, the bedroom door flew open and there a man stood, completely surprised. "Lay the fuck down!" I ordered. I took my pistol out of my holster and place it at his head and then threw him down to the floor. "Where's the dope and money?" I grilled him. "I don't know…I don't know what you're talking 'bout," he said frantically. I looked at Tiffany and whispered to her that I was going to kill her and then I hit the man in the head with my pistol. "Where's the dope and money," I for the second time. He kept yelling, frantically, that he didn't know what I was talking about. I told Tiffany to find something to tie him up with and then he screamed and tried to get up off the floor. I hit him on top of his head again with the pistol and blood shot all over the room The walls were spattered and he was bleeding profusely from his head, blood covering his entire face, dripping from the bottom of his chin. He was screaming so loud that I knew that the neighbors were able to hear him. To make matters worse, there were people outside when I walked up to the apartment initially. Finally, he lay down on the floor. I thought he was dead. I rushed over to Tiffany and grabbed her by her hair and drug her into the living room. I pointed my gun at her. "If I end up killin' this nigga, I'm goin' to kill you too hoe!" I told her in no uncertain terms. I didn't hear the man get up; however, I looked up and I saw that he had made his way to the kitchen towards where the back door was located. I heard the door open and I took my gun off of Tiffany and pointed it towards the direction of the kitchen. I saw him run past the back kitchen window, yelling, "Help! Help!"

Shit, this nigga done got away I thought to myself. I told Tiffany to put on her clothes and then we dipped out of the front door. There were neighbors all around looking at us as we ran out. My mask was still on my face; therefore, I knew that no one could finger me. That was not the case with Tiffany. She was not wearing a mask and she would be easily identifiable. Back in the woods, I took my off and my clothes because they had blood all over them. I hid my pistol in the grass and placed a brick on top of it behind the apartments. To this very day, I'm not sure what made me place my pistol in the grass. I just figured that if I got pulled over by the police as I left, they wouldn't find a gun in my possession. I told Tiffany to meet me out front, at the corner of the street that the shopping center parking lot was located on, and then I took off walking in the opposite direction towards the spot where I had parked my truck. I made it back to my truck without incident. I put the key in the ignition and started the truck. I shifted into and drive and I pulled out of the parking lot and drove to the designated corner where I had told Tiffany to me. I rolled the window down as I pulled up to Tiffany and instructed her, "Hurry up and get yo ass in the back and lay yo ass down." I was fighting-mad about what had occurred but thankful that I had gotten away. However, there was one pressing issue that I knew that I had to deal with; I had to go back and retrieve my pistol…but first I needed to go and change my clothes. Back at my apartment, I told Tiffany to take a shower in the guest bathroom and to give me the clothes that she had on. Then I went and showered in my bedroom. I got dressed and told Tiffany that I had to make a quick-run and instructed her to stay at my apartment until I got back. I took our blood-stained clothes, drove to a nondescript dumpster to dispose of the garments and then made my way back to the shopping center parking lot, in order to recover my pistol. Upon returning to the shopping center parking lot, I was blocked in by a Cobb County police cruiser *and* a City of Smyrna police cruiser. "Put your hands out of your driver-side window," the officer yelled through his speaker. I immediately began to cuss him out, informing him that, "I didn't so shit…what the fuck is goin' on!" A second officer walked up to the driver-side of my truck and pointed his gun at me. "Do not move!" he warned, as he opened my door and snatched me – face down – to the ground. I was informed that the authorities were looking for a robbery suspect that had been seen leaving the area in a black GMC Suburban and that my truck matched the description. The officer pulled me up off of the ground and began to question me. I told them that I was on my way to the studio and that I had decided to stop and grab something to eat on my way. I've always been a laid back type of cat, so I kept my cool. I asked the officer if it was alright for me to smoke and cigarette and he said, "Yeah, go ahead…that's fine." I pulled out a Newport and enjoyed the soothing feeling from the nicotine. As they searched my truck, a detective drove up with a witness sitting in the backseat of his gray, four-door, Crown Victoria. The detective ordered me to stand in front his vehicle, and I did. At least twenty minutes had passed and I was still in front of the detectives car; posing. "Turn the left…now to the right. Face straight forward," the detective kept repeating over and over. As much as I tried, I could not see the witness face, just their silhouette. Finally I said, "I know the law officer and if a witness can't identify the person within a certain timeframe, then you have to let me go. So let me go so I can go about my day." The officer walked over to me with a smirk on his face, read me my rights and place me in the back of his police cruiser but he never did handcuff me. The officer returned to my truck to search for evidence I assumed. I leaned over and got my phone off of my hip, called and Mike and let him know what was going on. I told him to go to the apartment and get rid of Tiffany.

I was taken back to Smyrna sub-station and questioned. The detective contacted Crystal and asked for her to come to the station so that the witness could verify whether or not she was the woman that was seen at the robbery earlier that day. The witness said indicated that Crystal was not the same woman that they had seen earlier and the detective told her that she was free to leave. I was cussing the officers during this entire time for putting my wife through this ordeal. A short time later I was taken over to the Cobb County Jail and booked. During processing I saw the same detective standing on the other side of a window with Tiffany. As soon as our eyes met, he walked around to me and stated in a manner as if he already knew the answer to his question, "Now, do you want to talk? We got your ass!"

"Like I told your ass before, you got the wrong person. Now get the fuck out my face!" I said confidently. He went back to Tiffany and they began to talk and then the both them walked outside. All I could think about was, "They got her and what the fuck is she telling him?"

The judge and the district attorney – the D.A. – knew that my attorney was out of town working on another case and he had informed Crystal that he would be in months' time. In spite of this fact, I was shuttled back and forth to court. However, during the interim, my attorney's assistant had come to the jail to meet with me. Nevertheless, I informed her that I preferred to speak with my attorney and not her. It was not anything personal against her, although I believe that she felt that it was. I don't think that she could fully appreciate the level of understanding that my lawyer and I had. Shit, I had been paying him on a regular basis for years, knowing that the lifestyle that I lived would more-then-likely lead me to require his services. I had dealt with my attorney much like a person that pays their car insurance premium. A person pays their car insurance for two reasons. First off, because it is required by law and secondly, they pay in case of the event of an accident – they're covered and therefore protected from certain degree of liability. I found irony in the fact that after all these years of "pre-paying", the one time that I needed him most – the motherfucker is out of town! I called Crystal and told her to find me another lawyer until my attorney returned. She asked me why I didn't want my attorney's assistant to tend to things and I told because I did not feel comfortable with her, Crystal hired me another lawyer. My first time in court with the new attorney and the judge granted me a bond. That motherfucker told the judge that I did not want a bond! I cussed his sorry-ass out in the courtroom while the judge simultaneously dismissed the bond that she had just offered to my attorney on my behalf. I fired the attorney right then and there; before the judge could bang her gavel and conclude my court hearing. I instructed Crystal to find and hire me another attorney and she informed me that our money was getting tight. "Isn't Mike giving you money?" I asked her. I had told Mike to get all of my dope from the apartment, sell it and to give Crystal the money. "No, I haven't heard from Mike," she replied.

Shortly thereafter, Crystal hired me another attorney. Upon our first meeting, he brought along my discovery file and he read everything that Tiffany had told the police. She had turned state's witness and agreed to testify against me. As if that wasn't enough fucked up news, he informed me that Tiffany had taken the detective to the location where I had left my pistol and that the police had it in their possession. I feeling of defeat was welling up inside of me and then he let me know that the police had been unable to obtain any fingerprints off of the pistol. That was a huge victory for me indeed. Yet, I knew that I was fighting an uphill battle. I told my newest attorney that I could still beat the case and I explained that in her statement, Tiffany had described my Suburban as being black and gray in color. But if she was indeed with me, as she had alleged, she would know that my truck was all black and not black and gray as she had communicated in her sworn statement. "That's a good point to put out there but she stills knows you," the attorney said flatly. Confident as ever, I said, "That's an easy one. Look...the judge and the district attorney already knows that I'm a drug dealer...so we can say that the reason why we know one another is because Tiffany used to buy drugs from me." Continuing on I explained, "When the detective asked Tiffany who was with her when the attempted robbery took place, she gave my name to keep the 'actual' person free and figured that I'd get locked up anyway."

Crystal brought Shelton to see me while I awaited my trial date. He had started to crawl and it seemed like I had missed so much time since I had been locked up on this charge. We talked about the things that we were going to do once I got out promised her that I was going to change and become a better man. That following morning, I was called to court. I informed the C.O. (corrections officer) that I was not due in court until two weeks later but I had to go anyway. However, instead of going into the courtroom, I was ushered into the judge's chambers. The D.A. was there, as was my attorney. It did not take the D.A. anytime at all before he announced, "Mr. Dickson, I summoned you and your lawyer here today to tell you that if you go to trial, you will win. However, before you walk out the court a free man, I will bring to the judges attention, the document you signed two years ago regarding your conviction on a weapons case stated that if you received another charge before the stated term imposed by the judge…that you would receive a fifteen year prison sentence. And now sir, you have received another charge *before* the stated terms expiration date. And when you beat your case, I *promise* you that you will receive those fifteen years in prison." Until that very moment, I had forgotten about that document that I had signed almost two years prior. But I still said to the D.A., "That's some bulllshit and I know I got the case beat and if you do bring up the document the judge might not go with what you're asking and I can still walk out of here a free man."

"No you won't Mr. Dickson. The judge has already agreed to honor the previous agreement and prison term. And furthermore, your upcoming trial is with the very same judge that you had two years ago that imposed the fifteen year sentence in the event that you received another charge. Therefore, I am offering you a plea. Fifteen years, of which you'll serve a maximum of five. You can accept the plea or you can be a dumb-ass and get the full fifteen. The choice is completely yours," the D.A. gleefully explained. I looked at the

District Attorney and then at my attorney. My attorney advised me that I should take the plea deal because they had me in a box. I asked the D.A. if I could use the phone to call my wife and he obliged. My attorney took out his cell phone and handed it to me. I called Crystal and explained the plea deal that had been offered. "I don't want to gamble with this Polo," Crystal said. "Crystal even though their trying to trap me up I got the case won and it's up to the judge to go along with the D.A," I countered. "I understand that Polo, but it's the same judge from two years ago that you have to go in front of. So I'd rather you do five years rather than fifteen years!" she pleaded. "Are you sure you want me to take the plea?" I asked Crystal. "Yes, do the five years and come back home to us, I love u," Crystal said.

"I love you too Crystal." I gave the phone back to my lawyer and I signed the plea deal for fifteen years, of which I would a maximum of five in state prison.

High Tower State Prison

Facing prison can be an extremely tumultuous time. It wasn't the first time that I would be locked up but this was my first time going to prison. I blocked out all the noise that surrounded me by focusing on those things that were most important in my life. Handcuffed and shackled, I arrived at High Tower State Prison (now known as Alfa State Prison ever the since the FEDS had came in and began investigating the numerous murders that had been occurring there.) I stepped off of the bus and planted my feet onto the soil of one of Georgia's most dangerous prisons. Revisiting days of the past for a second, I recalled hearing about the deaths and vicious attacks that took place on a daily basis in High Tower. Dating as far back to the 1970's I had been told when I was growing up. Stories spread all throughout the country about this prison and this was a place that you would *not* want to come to visit, *let alone* be incarcerated at. A good deal of that mayhem had calmed down but every now and again, shit is going to occur in any prison. I was placed in A-unit, a building where prisoners going through their diagnostic evaluation; prisoners that had good time and juveniles were housed. I continuously went back and forth to various doctors as they ran all kinds of tests on me. On my way back from one of my tests, I walked over to the prison store. During my walk over to the store, I began to see nigga's that I knew from the streets. "What up Polo!" said Que in his Jamaican accent? "What's up with you?" I shot back at him. Que walked up to me and I could smell the scent of weed coming off of his prison uniform. "Let me get some of that weed Que," I said. Que told me to wait outside of the gym and about ten minutes later he came back and handed me a dime bag of weed. "Hey Polo, this ain't shit like the quality of weed that you sold on the streets, but it's the best that I've got. You don't owe me nothing and whenever you need some more just holla at me nigga. One more thing I need to tell you. The word is out that you're here and a couple of pussy-ass nigga's are waiting for you to get through your diagnostic testing, because after testing, you gone be moved across the yard to the main prison. But these nigga's talking 'bout getting at you for the nigga's you got at out in the street. These nigga's up in here are busting' nigga's heads open, left and right...that's why I brought you this too!" Que handed me a knife. Quickly and carefully, I inconspicuously placed the shank in side of my pants and told him thanks for everything. I grabbed my bag of food that I had bought at the commissary and headed back towards A-unit.

Back in my cell I rolled up the weed and started smoking. It didn't take me long to get high and I began thinking about the life that I left behind in the real world. High as hell, I walked outside to the yard. I looked around and noticed that I was in an entirely different world. My new world consisted of razor-wire fences, guard towers occupied with officers holding high-powered rifles – ready to kill anyone that tried to escape. Next to me on the yard were a good number of juveniles. These young nigga's is one of the biggest reasons that High Tower *is* High Tower. A lot of the juvenile inmates are facing twenty and thirty years and a good number of them even have life sentences. They don't give a fuck about anything! They're some wild ass nigga's that indulge in homosexual acts. Once a juvenile reaches the age of eighteen, he is transferred across the yard to the main prison and then begins living amongst the rest of the prison population and that is when they really learn what they will be faced with.

I completed my diagnostic testing within two weeks and I was moved across the yard to the main prison and assigned to the C building, dorm sixteen. There were all types of faces looking at me, emitting mean-mugs and hardened stares. I was already known as a gang member, I had to look out for these nigga's, as well as the officers. I ran across a few people that I had known in the free world and some of them had turned into homosexuals and I made sure to keep my distance from them. The bell sounded signaling that it was time yard. Yard is basically where inmates are allowed to go outside to the "yard" and get some fresh air, among other things. I placed my things inside my footlocker and walked outside. There seemed to be roughly 300 inmates outside. Some played basketball, some messed around on the volleyball court and soccer field, while others just stood or sat around and chilled. I walked alone, as I always did and took off my shirt. I immediately felt the stares that were being projected my way. My "Gangsta" tattoo was visible as was my other tattoos and I had pretty good reason to believe that that was what they were staring at. I continued walking around and then I pulled out the blunt that I had rolled earlier in the day and took deliberate and strong pulls to inhale the smoke. I was preparing myself for anything that might go down. Thirty minutes later and yard was over. All of the inmates gathered in one big crowd and I knew that in a crowd such as this; anything was bound to pop off. I rested my hand on my knife that I had concealed in my pants and I was ready to put it to good use on any nigga that brought some bullshit my way. High from the weed that I had smoked, I walked over to the phone and called Crystal. She was livid! "Polo, don't you every scare me like that," Crystal snapped. "What are you talking about Crystal?" I asked. "You haven't called home in two weeks. I been worried about your ass, you know to call home every other day," Crystal instructed.

I started smiling and said, "Oh, you been worried about me boo, that's sweet."

"Polo, I just don't want anything to happen to you and I know your crazy ass," Crystal said matter-of-factly. "I'm going to make it home baby," I reassured Crystal.

My visit came at the end of my first week in the main prison from Crystal and Shelton. When I sat down in front of them, Shelton seemed scared to come to me. That damn-near broke my heart! I was tore up on the inside knowing that my own child was scared for me to hold him. He began to cry and I gently wiped the tears away from his eyes. "Polo," Crystal called out. I looked over at her and said, "Damn baby you're looking good!"

"Thank you," Crystal replied and began looking around. I could tell that something was bothering her and from the look on her face, I knew what it was. This was her first visit and she was extremely uncomfortable, as prison is not a comfortable environment to be in. I did not say anything to her about it. Instead, I began talking to my son, "Shelton, you know who I am?" Shelton shook his head yes. "Are you going to give Daddy a hug?" I asked and Shelton ran over to me. I picked him up and held tight. I didn't want to let him go. A few seconds later and Crystal asked Shelton if he was ready to go. I looked at her and asked, "Why are asking him that?" She told Shelton to give me a hug and then took him away from me, gave me a hug herself and said good bye. Crystal and Shelton walked out of the visiting room…neither of them looked back.

I returned to my dorm and started playing poker, trying to get my mind off of my visit from Crystal and Shelton and all the other shit that I had on my mind. Due to my lake of attention, I ended losing the hand and along with the loss, I owed $40 to the cats that I was playing against. One of my homeboy's walked up to me and saying, "Nigga you know you can't win when you playing with sissies. All them gay ass nigga's got *punk* luck." His statement added insult to injury and I was even more irritated about losing my money. However, I'm a real nigga and a real nigga pays the debt that he owes. I went to my cell, retrieved my money and the paid the punk. After settling up my debt, I walked to the restroom and smoked a blunt. It was hot as the Sahara inside the dorm. The temperature hovered somewhere around 102 degrees so I decided to make a Bombay to sip on. Now a Bombay is a concoction of coffee, Kool-Aid, jolly ranchers and pop (soda) and it is good as fuck! As if the heat wasn't overwhelming enough, the bugs flying and crawling only made things worse. All of the shit that was going on around me; the prison lifestyle in general was propelling me into a state of depression. The thought of suicide crossed my mind, primarily because I realized that I had abandoned my wife and son; the two most important people in my life. I'm sad to say that it had taken my incarceration to fully understand and finally accept the hurt that I had caused Crystal and Shelton, but especially Crystal and it devastated me. Feeling drained, I stretched out on my bunk and went to sleep. Sometime around 2am, a C.O. came to my cell and woke me up. He told me that I had gotten place on kitchen detail and that I needed to report to work immediately. I got myself together and headed out towards the kitchen. I walked up the hill that lead to the building where the kitchen was located, smoking on Newport. I gazed up into the pitch-dark sky and began to talk to God. I arrived at the kitchen to find a group of nigga's gathered around the officer's restroom, gawking downward at the wet floor. I would soon find out that the floor was wet due to the fact that it acted like a mirror because you could see the reflection from the wet floor. These nigga's used the floor to look up the female's skirts as they entered and exited the restroom. A couple of hours later we began to serve breakfast. My job was to pass trays down the line to the inmates that were being served. An inmate walked up to a group of cats that were moving down the line getting their food and said, "Hey, y'all nigga's was right! That bitch does give good head…that bitch sucked the shit outta my dick!" The nigga's that he was talking to all responded in staggered unison, "We told you that bitch is off the chain with it!" Naturally, I assumed that these fools were talking about one of the female officers until I heard one of them announce that, "The bitch is walking through the line right now!" I glanced over to see the female officer that they were talking about but I did so in a manner that was unnoticeable. I was shocked when I saw another inmate bend down and blow a kiss at them. "These some sick ass nigga's in here!" I thought to myself and I couldn't wait until I got the hell out of here. I was mumbling to myself in astonishment and then I looked at them nigga's and said pokerfaced, "All you nigga's need to die." Each of them stared at me and as I did them, unflinching. There was an officer standing nearby that must have sensed that there was something about to go down because he told me to go back to my dorm and I walked out of the kitchen, unnerved. Later that night, I went to take a shower and walked in on a nigga that I had known in the streets and he was getting fucked in his ass. I promptly turned around and went back to my cell. I could not believe what I had just witnessed. About forty minutes later, the guy that I had known in the streets came over to me and asked, "Polo, can I holler at you?"

"What the fuck you want nigga?!" I said. "This is me Polo. This is my life. I got caught up in the prison shit and I can't see my way out. I got twenty years to do…" I interrupted him, "Nigga that don't mean shit to me! You 'round here talking all that hard shit and then I walk in on you and you takin' dick in the ass."

"I got turned out Polo," he pleaded. "Pussy-nigga ain't no such thing of getting turned out…you wanted that shit from the start and since you saying that you so real, have you let your people know on the streets that you're a punk?" I asked. He looked at me with the sad-face and then walked away. His body language told the entire story. His secret was out. While he was still without earshot, I yelled out, "Tell your folks that you getting fucked in your ass nigga…because I will when I get out this mothafucka!"

A couple weeks later, I was outside in the yard smoking a blunt with some nigga's that I had known when I was out in the world. I couldn't help but notice some of the sick-ass games that some of the inmates were playing with one another. They would walk around and grab each other's dicks. I could not believe the shit that I was seeing. They would actually walk up to each other, and one would grab the other's dick squeeze it and then yank it down until the inmate fell down. The inmate on the ground would get up and do the same to the other inmate. I even saw some nigga's that used the sheets from their bed as picnic blankets and they'd lay them down and chill with other men like two lovers. The most disgusting shit that I saw occurred while I was on my way to take some food trays to the hole. I walked through a puddle of blood that had run out from one of the cells. I peeped into the cell and saw a man that had cut his dick off with a shaving razor. He was yelling out frantically, "I don't want it no more, I don't need it!" When the C.O. arrived at the bleeding man's cell, his dick was in one hand and the razor blade was in the other. In High Tower, games were not to be played. Playing a game could cause the end of your life with the quickness and your 2-3 year sentence could easily be converted into a life if you ended up having to kill a nigga. It was wise to refrain from silly games. That would help your chances of making it back home to your family alive, in one piece, as a man. I recall how this one particular nigga had raped the old woman that worked in the prison library and disfigured her face. As soon as the word got out that he had committed the brutal attack, some nigga's had him killed. When he raped that old woman, he essentially signed his own death warrant.

Back inside my cell, I went to sleep. After some time had passed, I was awoken by the tapping of my foot by a female C.O. Not realizing what was going, I jumped up and grabbed my knife, looking at her I was a crazed animal. She saw the knife and jumped back like she was scared as hell. "Bitch don't ever do that shit." I barked at her. "I'm sorry I just wanted to talk to you," she said apologetically. "About what?!" I said. "You know what," and then she looked down at my dick. "Bitch I'm not gone fuck you. I'm married. Plus you not my type and you 'round here giving these gay ass nigga's pussy and you don't even know that their fucking these punks up in here. You need to get checked for aids!" I told her. She got mad and said, "Shut the fuck up! Be careful 'round here. I'll lock your ass in the hole *or* get you fucked up!" She walked off and I lay back down and went back to sleep. It was easy to get pussy in prison. The women correction officers fuck for money or jewelry and many will fuck just because they think a nigga look good. One of the craziest things that I saw was nigga's that would masturbate to a woman that was fully-dressed. I never understood how a fully-dressed woman could get them off. I just couldn't understand that shit. These nigga's had all kinds of ways to masturbate too. Some of them would tie one end of a string around their dick and then tie the other end of the string around their foot. While they spoke to a female C.O., they would tap their foot and the string would pull their dick. They would repeat this process in order to cause the string to move in an up and down motion until they busted a nut. Then they would walk away from the officer, giddy over the fact that they believed that she never knew that she had just gotten them off.

Eolian State Prison

After five or six months, on a blistering-sunny day in July, I was transferred to Eolian State Prison. I stepped out of the prison van and two officers escorted me to the Warden Boscoe's office. I was questioned by one of the units' mangers and by the captain. Along with the questioning they took pictures of my tattoos and they paid special attention two in particular: the one on my stomach that read, "Gangsta": and the other that read, "Original". The unit manger opened up my file and said, "Mr. Dickson, I see here that you're an Original and a known gang member who is highly respected in prison. Now I need to ask you; are you going to start a gang war here at my prison?" I looked at him and said, "Sir, what are you talking about?"

"I need you to assure me that you will not cause a war here," the unit manager said.

"Like I said, what are you talking about?" I replied. The captain interrupted and yelled out, "No gang activity Mr. Dickson!"

"Look, I haven't gang banged since I was seventeen. Plus, I have a wife and a son at home waiting on me and another thing Georgia... ain't got no gangs," I informed them.

I ran across some Los Angeles Crips while I was at Eolian. One was a Rollin' Sixty and the other was a Rollin' Twenty. When I was banging I represented the "Original". On the streets, we would have all been enemies; however, on the inside there wasn't any "set trip-ping, we were all cool.

I called Crystal and I could feel the separation between us. Our conversations had become much different as she would be very short with me. I ended my call and starting playing dominoes with this cat from Chicago that we called "Chi" (pronounced Shy) and one of my homeboy's named YB. YB approached Chi and asked him some headphones that he had let him borrow that Chi had broken. The casual conversation led to an argument and YB pulled out a knife. Chi got so scared that he walked away in a hurried pace and went and sat on his bunk, shaking like a little bitch. YB asked me to go with him to see a white cat named Jimmy. Jimmy was the guy that had supposedly fixed YB's headphones after Chi had broken them. YB asked Jimmy if he had indeed fixed the headphones for Chi and he replied, "Yes." After verifying Chi's story we walked back over to Chi's cell to let him know that everything was cool. A C.O. saw us speaking with Chi and yelled over the intercom, "Lock down, lock down!"

"We ain't locking down shit!" we yelled back. In the snap of a finger, there were a gang of correctional officers, along with the cap-tain walking down the hallway. When they reached Chi's cell, where were congregated, they pleaded with us to lock down which required every inmate to go into their cell indefinitely. After a brief reluc-tance, we all returned to our cells.

I started going to school so that I could earn my GED. After a week of classes, I was taken over to Haynes State Prison for the GED test. I passed the test and was issued my certificate which I mailed home to my wife. I also volunteered for the self-help classes, substance abuse one-on-one, victim impact and alcoholic anony-mous. I wasn't required to take any of these classes, nor did I feel that I need any of them – I signed up for them on my own. My plea did not allow for parole but I thought that it wouldn't hurt to participate in the classes. You never knew what was going to happen in prison. In the event that I would be eligible for parole, I wanted to increase my chances of earning it. Completing these programs made it seem as if an inmate was "rehabilitated". Taking these classes also seemed to make the time go by faster. The busier I kept my mind, the better off that I was and I actually learned a thing or two from some of the programs. After returning to the dorm from one of my GED classes, I decided to call Crystal but I didn't get an answer. I kept calling back but still she didn't answer the phone. Finally, after roughly thirty minutes of calling, Crystal answered the phone, "What the fuck do you want Polo?" she angrily asked. "Why in the hell you can't answer the phone?" I said, "Because I'm busy!" Crystal told me.

"Look, I need to talk to your ass. When you coming to see me?" I asked Crystal. "I don't know," she replied. Suspicious, I asked, "Who you fuckin' Crystal?" "What!" she asked as if she was caught off guard. "Bitch, you heard me! Who you fucking?" I asked again. Crystal hung up the phone on me. My mind was going a-mile-a-minute and images of my past wrongs flickered through my thoughts. I begin remembering in detail, all of the arguments that Crystal had, specific things that were said, the women that I had gotten caught up with, the shootouts, slapping Misty and her abortion, the hurt that I had caused my family, Shelton's birth, our wedding day. I threw the phone into the wall and walked back to my cell. I could feel the stares upon me but I couldn't see anything but red and the only thing that I could hear were the thoughts that rambled inside of my head. I was in a bad place mentally and it seemed like everybody knew it. Not long after Crystal had hung up on me, I got sentenced to the hole. For some reason, the captain believed that I was somehow the cause of a fight that I had absolutely nothing to do with. You know how the saying goes…"when it rains, it pours." It felt like I was paying penance for all the dirt that I had done and for the next three months I sat in solitary confinement for 23 hours a day and the few privileges that were allowed in prison were taken away from me.

———— ⬤ ————

I started cutting hair in the barbershop when my sentence in solitary was completed. Things got a lot better after I began cutting hair. I built a good rapport with the C.O.'s while I worked as a barber. I would cut their hair and the would bring me "free" world food, like McDonald's or Wendy's and even liquor to drink on sometimes. I started paying one particular C.O. seventy-five dollars every week and the hoe would bring me a half-gallon of E & J or Hennessy. I sold caps, which were half a shot for five dollars to make my money. I'd look out for the handful of nigga's that I was cool with and then I would drink the rest.

YB introduced me to this cat named Low Key. He was a cool ass nigga. The funny thing is, YB and Low Key were Gangster Disciples, also known as GD's and I was a Original. Original's and GD's were enemies; however, we were mad cool with each other. I really experienced racism at Eolian State Prison. When it was time to go to chow and eat; white prisoners sat on one side of the cafeteria and black inmates sat on the other side of the cafeteria. The C.O's were racist as hell at Walker too. They talked to us any old kind of way and that was the main reason that I kept getting sent back to the hole. I didn't give a fuck about a C.O. I refused to be disrespected. Another crazy about this prison was the fact that it housed a large number of child molesters. I would estimate that about 75% of the prison population was indeed serving time for child molestation. They had a look about themselves. It seemed like you could tell who they were by simply looking at them. What was really fucked up is that many of the child molesters were serving short, 2 to 3 years sentences whereas a drug dealer would be serving out a 15 year to life sentence. I can't tell you much about any other state but in Georgia, the laws are fucked up once were in the Georgia Department of Corrections system, they tried their best to keep you there.

I brought in the 2003 New Year with news from the parole board informing me that I would have to max out my sentence. Georgia had implemented some bullshit-ass law that required violent offenders to serve out at least 75% of their sentence. That law nullified a large number of inmates from being granted parole. The effects from the new law were also felt on the county level as well. The county jails suffered from overcrowding as inmates had to wait for a bed to open at one of the state prisons. Instead of granting parole to alleviate the problem of overcrowding, inmates suffered and the billion-dollar prison system displayed its true colors as it sought out profit rather than justice.

Stressed out in delving deeper in the abyss of depression, I continued to do my time alone. I still had not heard a peep from Crystal. She hadn't accepted any of my calls nor had she come to visit me. She did, however, send an occasional letter and put some money in my commissary. I started getting into verbal confrontations with a lot of different inmates. I damn-near got into a fight with some Muslims cats and with another group of fake-ass nigga's that was claiming Crip. They didn't know a damn thing about "Crippin'"; how the gang started, about the hoods out in Los Angeles or about the blue color that we claim and its' origin. I gambled every day to try and make the days pass as quickly as possible. At night I would lay in my bunk, crying from the pain that was seeping out of me. Later that week Crystal and Shelton came to visit me. Shelton fell asleep in my arms as I held him and for a few seconds everything in the world was alright. This gave me an opportunity to speak to Crystal. "So, where you been Crystal?" I asked. "Polo, I don't want to talk about it right now,"

Crystal said as she rolled her eyes. "Tell me who you been fucking?" I demanded. Stone-faced, Crystal looked me square in my face and replied, "Nobody Polo!" I wasn't convinced; however, I thought it best to change the subject because I did not want to get into an argument with her. Unbeknownst to me, I must have struck a nerve with Crystal because she began to go off, "You think I enjoy this? Coming up in here to see you, touching you and knowing once I walk out that you have to stay here. You think I enjoy hearing our son asking me where is his daddy? I don't enjoy any of this shit Polo! I hate it *and* I hate you so much right now. You left us and every day I tell Shelton that you love him so much and that you're a good father to him. I keep you in his mind because that's my responsibility as a woman, a mother and a wife. It hurts for me to come up here and see you like this, that's why when I do visit I can't stay no longer than thirty minutes!"

"I'm sorry Crystal," I said. "Yeah, I know you are," Crystal reassured me and then keeping with her routine, she and Shelton left within her thirty timeframe.

My problems with other inmates and once again I was placed in the hole while I was being investigated for supposedly stealing things out of some white boy's locker; at least that's what he had told the C.O.'s. I served the standard 90 days in solitary and then I was returned to general population, also referred to as, Gen Pop. Immediately upon my return, I noticed that something had drastically changed at Eolian State Prison. The majority of prisoners were using cocaine. I estimated that as much as 90% of the prison was abusing cocaine. I knew the habits and side effects from being addicted to cocaine from my days of pushing the drug over on Franklin Road in Marietta. I could tell that inmates were "joneing" for the drug, I didn't have to actually see them using the cocaine – I knew that they were on it. Allegedly, an inmate that was working on a detail at the Georgia State Patrol gained access to the evidence room, lifted a kilo of cocaine and smuggled it back into Eolian State Prison. Within two weeks of the cocaine epidemic, large numbers of inmates were either reassigned to different dorms or transferred to other prisons, including me.

Fellow State Prison

I did not know what to expect as I traveled to Fellow State Prison in June of 2004. When I arrived, the very first thing that I noticed is that the prison appeared to be extremely laid back. A lot of the inmates wore Timberland boots and I felt a small sense of freedom that I had not experienced while I was at High Tower or Eolian State Prisons. The food at Fellow State Prison was remarkably different too; in a good way. It didn't feel like a prison at all. Or should I say that it did not feel like a "real" prison. I was directed to my dorm and taken to the bed that I had been assigned. I put my things up and I asked a few nigga's that were standing nearby, "How is shit in here?" Each of them informed me, as a collective, that Fellow State Prison was the best place to be if you were serving time in the Georgia Department of Corrections. There was plenty of dope on the inside and a couple of nigga's had cell phones too. Hearing that, I knew just what I had to do. I asked a nigga named Mike if I could use his cell phone. Mike appeared to be a decent nigga and agreed to my request. I called Mike and instructed him to bring me an ounce of weed and a cell phone. Two days later, Mike came to the prison for a visit. I needed a mule, so I paid and arranged for someone to bring me the cell phone. I had to draft up a different scheme to get the weed inside. Incarcerated at Fellow State Prison and already I had things moving. It felt like every nigga in there was trying to figure out who the fuck I was. I met a nigga named Twan and I explained to him that I would hit him off with a quarter-once of weed he could get the dope inside of the prison for me. The plan seemed infallible; however, on the day that he was supposed to smuggle the weed into the prison, he informed me that the weed appeared to have been stolen because he said that it was no longer in the spot where Mike had left it. I put my cell phone up and got up in his face. "Nigga I'll kill you if you trying to hold out on my dope!" About five minutes later some other nigga walks up to us and says, "I know who stole your weed and I'll show you who it is.: he made clear. As I walked to the dorm where the perpetrator was housed, I looked behind me and noticed that I had about five or six nigga's following me. I abruptly, turned around and asked, "What the fuck y'all doing?" They explained to me that they would handle this nigga for me, if anything jumped off. I did not know these nigga's from a can of paint but they all said how much they were amazed and they respected the fact that I had been at the prison less than a week, and already I had a cell phone and some weed. I figured that they're thinking was that I would look out for them in the end. As I entered the dormitory and approached this nigga's bed, I saw that he was rolling about a half-ounce of weed. "Nigga you know that's my shit," Twan barked as he got in the guy's face. The nigga didn't back down, he started talking shit before I interrupted both of them, "Look playa, you don't know me and I don't know you but that weed you stole from Twan…it ain't, that shit is mine. That means that you stole it from me!" I said. I tried to be politically correct in my explanation, "Now, y'all all now that just got here and I don't know shit 'bout what y'all do here, but *you* need to give me my shit before I whoop your ass!"

"Man, I'm telling you. My sister dropped this off to me last night. She only brought me a quarter and that's what you see me rolling up…I don't know why Twan is saying that I took your shit but if you ask me, I think Twan the one that really got your shit and he just trying to put it off on me," the cat said. I looked at Twan and said, "I'll be right back" and took off walking towards my dorm. I went to my locker and took off my lock. As I turned around to head back to dorm where Twan and everybody else was waiting, Mike came over to me and said, "Polo, let me holla at you homie."

"What do you want Mike?" I asked, irritated. "Man, look…you just got here and when I saw you talking to Twan 'bout bringing your weed in here for you, I wanted to tell you then that you shouldn't fuck with that nigga. Now I see you got your lock in your hand and you 'bout to go back over there and fuck some nigga's up! But these white folks don't play that shit in here! This is a county camp prison homie…and if you fuck a nigga up…they will press charges against you and give your ass some more time!"

I walked away from Mike without responding and went back over to the other dorm but the door to get in was locked. I tapped on the glass on the lock and all of those nigga's started looking worried. "Count time!" an officer yelled and I hurried back to my bunk so that I would not receive an infraction for being out of place. During count, I kept thinking to myself about the weed situation and I decided that I was not going to do anything to the nigga Twan or the nigga that he alleged had stolen from me; my reason being that I knew that I would be hit with more time if I had put my hands on either one of those nigga's. Therefore, I charged it to the game because a once of weed was not worth me doing more time.

———— ◆ ————

Crystal was on the phone telling me that she wanted a divorce and about the different people that she was sleeping with. She was saying some real hurtful shit and I deep down I believed that she was trying to hurt me on purpose and she was succeeding. After all, she told me all of these things on my birthday. I ended the call and put my cell phone up in my secret hiding; the floor drain, because cell phones were considered contraband. Over and over I asked God, "Why?" My time was short now and I would be a free man real soon yet all I could think about were the visions of Crystal having sex with some other man. Flashes of her naked body, her facial expressions and her sounds of pleasure ran rampant in my mind. It was tormenting! I prayed and fasted to get closer to God and still I could find no peace within myself. My spirit was dead. A week or so later I received the divorce papers. I read each word in a deliberate manner but it was not until my eyes saw the signature line with Crystal's Derrick Hancock written on it – the bitter reality set in. I called her immediately and she told me to sign the papers so that things would not be so hard for her. "I'm not signing shit!" I told her. She got mad and starting telling me about the some nigga who asked her to marry him and how Shelton had called another nigga "Daddy". I studied every word, each syllable. I internalized everything that Crystal told me and I said to her, "I love you still."

On July 7th, 2004, Crystal went to court and the judge granted her the divorced that she desired. I spoke with her later that afternoon and I could hear the sadness in her voice. "If you would have sent the judge or the lawyer a letter saying that you didn't want the divorce, the judge wouldn't have granted me the divorce," Crystal said in a gloomy tone. She was awarded sole custody of Shelton and it felt like my world had ended.

A Letter from a Stranger

B ack in the hole, I received from the living dead; a stranger in my eyes. The letter was from Tiffany and in it she explained to the reason why she had turned state's evidence and agreed to testify against me. She said that there was not any dope or money in the apartment to begin with. I had been set up, but for a reason. Tiffany had lied about the entire scenario. Tiffany explained that she had strategically invented the lick because she figured that I would have killed whoever was in the apartment once I discovered that there wasn't any dope or money there. By her account, she had been raped by several men that lived at the apartment and she wanted them killed. I wondered to myself why Tiffany had not simply gone to the police and reported the rape but that very question was addressed a little further down in the letter. Apparently, Tiffany had warrants and feared being arrested so she chose not to report the rapes. She inquired about Crystal and Shelton's well-being and apologized for being the reason that I had been taken away from them and incarcerated. Tiffany pleaded for my forgiveness and ended the letter with a sincere apology. My entire body shook with anger before exploding in rage. I began kicking my door and throwing shit about the cell, acting deranged. It was a true example of an out-of-body experience. For a few minutes I saw myself in a demented state as if there was two of me in the dreary, undersized, one-man cell.

TRUTH

I bounced back and forth, in constant turmoil; fighting in my mind about my circumstance. I prayed to God to help me to a righteous path of life and asked if He could provide me with an escape route so that I could finish running my prison marathon. I had been running in place in prison for over fours and I felt like I was ready to give up. I dropped to my knees and asked God to carry me to the finish line of freedom. I could not imagine a better prize.

The Trap

The deputy warden called me into his office and told me to have a seat. "Mr. Dickson," he said. "Yes sir," I answered. "Are you ready to go home?" the deputy warden asked as he sat up in his black, leather, ergonomic chair. "Sir, you know I am, but why are you asking me that?" I asked with a puzzled look on my face. "Mr. Dickson, I'm not here to bullshit you," he said. "And...if you can give me what I want, such as information, there's a great deal waiting for you on the other end of this phone. I'll call down to Atlanta and have them process your release paperwork ASAP." He sat back in his seat, interlocked his fingers together and looked at me with a determined look in his eyes. "Information," I repeated with a chuckle. "Deputy warden, I don't have no information for you," I explained.

"Think about it for a minute Mr. Dickson. I can have you home with your wife and son by weeks end. You do know that I know about everything that goes in my prison, don't you?" he asked. "I also know about every inmate in my prison; their case, their sentence, their wife's, their girlfriends, their kids...I even know who's fuckin' who in this prison Mr. Dickson!" the deputy warden said in a convincing manner.

"No I don't," I interrupted. "Sure you do son. Let me ask you this – how many cell phones have I taken you?" he said. "None," I shot back. "You're absolutely right Mr. Dickson. I didn't actually recover them off of your person. However, I do know that they were yours…and if you were to get charged and convicted of possession of an escape device that I could place a ninety-day extension on your sentence," the deputy warden assured me. I thought to myself, *mothafucka, I done did almost five fuckin' years…ninety more days ain't shit!* "So what the hell you saying? For your information, the parole board ain't gone give me parole…they been told me that I'm gone max out…so that bullshit ninety-day extension ain't bout shit," I said, pissed that he would even approach me about some snitch shit. "You have to get home to put your marriage back together right? Oh, I *was there* when the sheriff served you with your divorce papers…do you remember? Also, Mr. Dickson, be aware that I do know you have another cell phone in my prison right now," he assured me. "What I want to know is; how are all the phones and the drugs getting in here? I promise that you will be released from my prison by weeks end if you are willing to provide me with this information," he continued. "There is one more thing that I need to know. Who is the person or persons that have been dumpster diving to obtain senior citizens bank information and stealing funds out of their accounts?" the deputy warden concluded. What type of nigga does this asshole think I am I thought to myself. I started laughing at him, then said, "If you know our cases like you said you do; then you know full and well that I'm in prison purely because somebody *snitched* on me and I hate *snitches* and you *know* I'm not a snitch! I don't know shit 'bout no money being stole, about no phones or nothing else you talking about!" I said angrily. "One more thing sir…my wife and son is none of your damn business…now, are we done?" I asked. I wanted to smack the shit out of the deputy warden for even approaching me with this bitch-shit.

"You just made your time here harder son. Now, get the hell out my office!" he proclaimed.

Outside on the yard I was lifting weights, trying to get shit off of my mind when the pastor of the Church in the Valley came and asked me to go with him to the chow hall. We were greeted by another pastor when we arrived at the chow hall. The pastor ordained me as a Deacon. Even though I'm a thug-ass nigga, I *still* know the Bible and the Lord had blessed with a gift. When I spoke the Word, people would accept it as the truth and they respected me. Numerous pastors had invited me to speak at their church once I was released and said that I would be a blessing to a lot of people. That made me feel good, although I never went and spoke in front any congregations. It made me feel like my life was worth something.

Amiss State Prison

"**P**ut your hands on the side of your fucking pants and look down and don't say shit!" yelled one of the Correctional Emergency Response Team (CERT) officers. I didn't pay their orders any attention. I grabbed my property and walked over to a table where another officer was doing inventory. The officer recorded all of my property and then looked at his clipboard and found my name on the roster sheet. "You're about to go home. All you have to do while you're here is complete the pre-transitional program, stay out of trouble and you'll be out of here on your way to a half-way house in no time. I see that you're in a gang. Don't get caught up in that shit while you're here. I want to see you go home when you're supposed to," the officer told me. "Thank you sir," I said.

By this time in my bid, the state of Georgia had converted High Tower State Prison to house female inmates. Therefore, this caused a lot of cats to be transferred over to Amiss. I already knew that I was going to see a lot of nigga's that I knew. Amiss didn't seem to be much different from any other prison that I had been in. These nigga's didn't give shit about anything either. I left my cell and walked over to speak with the unit manager. He explained the pre-transitional program to me. Basically, the program last twelve weeks twelve and I would be going outside of the prison working on one of the details. In the evenings, I would come back to the prison and take classes related to the program. Primarily, the state wanted to assess if you were ready to be placed back in society.

Shortly after starting the program, the entire prison was placed on quarantine due to a medical crisis. Somehow, the medical staff had erroneously allowed an inmate into the general population that had tuberculosis (TB) and he had infected numerous inmates and it was turning into a pandemic. The Center for Disease Control and Prevention (CDC) had come into the prison and complete an investigation. Every inmate was tested, along with all of the C.O.'s and all the other members of the prison staff. In a nutshell, anybody that may have come into contact with one of the infected inmates was tested. There were multiple news stories reporting about the TB outbreak at Amiss. There was so much of an uproar that it was being reported that the CDC wanted residents of Pelham, the small town where the prison is located, to be tested as well. During a period of quarantine, transfers are not allowed; in or out. Because of this, the pre-transitional program was placed on hold. That meant that some of the people would be extended past the required twelve weeks.

When the CDC finally completed their investigation and cleared the prison to be taken off of quarantine lock-down, transfers were once-again taking place. We all assumed that the first prisoners to be released would be those inmates that had been extended past their twelve weeks for the pre-transitional release program. However, we were wrong. That was not the case at all and when the first transfer after the quarantine took place, I was included. I was getting out of prison and heading to a half-way house.

Marshall Fall Transitional Center

D amn, it felt good to be back in the A! I was back in the city that I claim but it still felt like I was standing on a banana peel. I had one foot out of prison but I it felt as if I was standing on a banana peel...one mistake and I would be going right back to the penitentiary. However, I was one big step closer to being a free man and no longer a part of the Georgia Department of Corrections. Marshall Fall T.C., as I called it, had just turned into a transitional center. It was a diversion center for those on probation. Crystal brought me some of my clothes. I had to get my shit together quick because the following morning I had a pass to leave the center to begin job searching.

The next morning, I got up and put on my clothes; fresh from head to toe. I went outside and waited at the bus stop which was situated in between the women's side of the halfway house and the side that I was staying on; the men's side. The Marta pulled up to my stop. I stepped up onto the bus, paid my fare and took a seat. I chose to sit closer to front because I wanted to make sure that I could see as much shit as possible. I had not been in the world in over 4 years. I was excited to be out of prison. Most of the men and women from Marshall Fall sat together on the bus. A few of them sat all the way to the back so that they could fuck or get some head. I rode the bus until it had reached near downtown and then I got off and walked.

Looking around, I saw that not much had changed since I had been away. There were a few new buildings scattered about and I noticed that one or two project complexes had been razed and it seemed as though a lot of people that walked around were zombies. I couldn't see any life in them. They looked like the unhappiest motherfuckers on the planet! The biggest change that I notice while walking around downtown was the prolific presence of gay men. These gay men had mouths full of gold teeth and they appeared to be between 17 and 20 years old. I wandered aimlessly around until it was time for me to return to the center. I had received the pass to go and seek out employment but in all actually, I had used my time to look over the landscape of things so that I wouldn't get caught up at the center when I did my own shit.

Still Fucking Up

I met my ex-wife at Cumberland Mall in Marietta and I told her that I needed to go on an interview at a staffing service in Marietta. She drove me to the interview and upon my return to the car after the interview I could tell in her body language that something was wrong. She looked over at me and handed me my phone book. It took me by surprise because I thought that my phone book was in my pocket. Apparently, it had fallen onto the floor when I got out of the car for my interview. I knew Crystal like the back of both my hands, so I already knew what she was thinking and I also knew exactly what the impending conversation was going to be about. We rode in an awkward silence until she began shaking her head and smacking her teeth. "Crystal," I blurted out forcefully. "It's over Polo," Crystal responded. "Look Crystal I haven't called any of these bitches!" I explained. "You're lying!" Crystal shouted. "I'm not going to argue with you," I said in a calm tone and I did not say another word the rest of the ride. Crystal me off at the bus station but before I could get out of the car she said, "Seeing those numbers in your book was like a big slap in the face Polo. You know how hard it was for me to let my guard down and let you back in and to start over like nothing ever happened." I could hear the pain in her voice and it rocked me to my core. "Crystal, I told you that I haven't called any of these bitches!" I responded. "Why are you still telling lies, Polo?"

Crystal asked. The conversation was turning into an argument and I felt myself getting pissed. "How the fuck you figure I'm lying to your motherfucking ass Crystal?" I hollered. "Because I called every last single one of those numbers and some hoe answered every time!" Crystal spouted. "That don't mean shit!" I countered. I knew that I was lying my ass off but she would never know the truth unless I told her I figured. "Polo I wouldn't be mad if these were new female's numbers that you had, but these are the same bitches that you slept with during our marriage." Crystal said in an exasperated voice.

"Now you're lying'! Old females…new females…you ass would still be mad!" I said. Crystal had set straight up in her seat and turned to me. "OK, I want you to erase all of those numbers and I don't ever want you to talk to any of them again. It's me and *only* me." Crystal had dug her heels in and gave an ultimatum.

"Alright then Crystal, you win," I said. "Hell nawl Polo…promise me."

"I promise Crystal," I responded.

I'm Being Talked About

I'm in a routine now. I would wake up, take my shower, get myself together and get dressed. This particular morning, I hopped on the bus headed out for an interview. I took the bus to the MLK Center where I met my aunt Joy. We hung out for a little while before she dropped me off for my interview. The interview went well but I was pressed for time. I was supposed to meet up with Crystal and Shelton but it didn't look like I would be able to, so I decided to walk around downtown for a little while. After some time had passed, I got back on the bus and headed back to the center. I sat next to a woman that was a resident at the Metro halfway house. "Hey, you from the halfway house across the street from us right?" she asked. I looked at her distrustfully and replied, "Yeah, why?"

"Cause every woman over there is talking about you. Every day they ask each other if anyone has seen you, and the ones that do see you, they all say that you so fine. Every day you walk out the center, you be looking good with some fresh shit on!" the woman told me. "How you know it's me their talking about?" I asked. She laughed and said, "Cause when you got on the bus one day, five girls from the center said, 'there he is.'" I scanned the bus to a quick once-over and saw the women that the lady was talking about. Each one of them smiled at me and a couple even winked their eye and another two blew me a kiss. This was some crazy shit. Thing is, these women been in prison just like me and sex on the top of their priority list too…along with getting out of the halfway house.

The Holidays

Due to the holiday season the Superintendent and the Job Coordinator had stopped us from going out searching for jobs and going on any interviews. Once the New Year had come in, we would be allowed to continue the process.

Christmas morning 2005, I was granted my first pass to go home. Crystal came to pick me up from Marshall Falls. My pass stipulated that I was allowed six hours with my family. I chose to leave the center at 2pm which meant that I did not have be back until 8pm.

Crystal's father and I had a deep and meaningful conversation in the living room and I have to admit, it was the epitome of a man-to-man dialogue. Crystal's father spoke bluntly about his expectations for Crystal and Shelton and I assured him that I was a man of word and that I would provide for my family and stay clear of any trouble. Afterwards, I made my upstairs and Crystal's mother, Brianna called me to her room. Brianna had handed me a gift and told me to open it. It was an $800.00 cashmere coat. I thanked her and gave an enormous and loving hug. Crystal walked in and pulled me to her room and handed me her gift to me. She also handed me a gift from her older sister, Janay. "Janay?" I said back to Crystal while I opened the gift. I was completely shocked that Janay would give me anything, let alone a Christmas gift due to the fact that we had never gotten along. By my account, the last conversation that the two of us had

had ended with me calling Janay a bitch. She had disapproved of Crystal dating from day one; not to mention marrying me. Truth be told, I had always looked at Janay as my sister in the same way that I had viewed Britney, Crystal's younger sister. Janay and I had a love/hate type of relationship. I looked at Crystal and she had the sweetest smile on her face. She leaned in closer to me and we shared a passionate kiss. I got up off the bed and walked over to Shelton's room. His room was a mess so I started cleaning up. He walked in and out of the room, looking at me and smiling. "Polo, your mother is on the phone...she wants to talk to you," Crystal told me. "Hell nawl!" I snapped. Crystal pleaded with me to speak with my mother and after some prodding, I conceded. Our conversation was extremely short and handed the phone back to Crystal. I finished straightening up Shelton's room which had taken me a little over an hour before Crystal told me to take shower. There was more company coming arriving at her parents' house. As the water from the shower poured down on my body, Crystal was putting on her make up. We talked about the vacation that we were going to take once I was finally done serving out the remainder of my sentence.

The family was all downstairs and we were all taking pictures, laughing, joking and having a good time. Janay had noticed the change in Crystal's disposition and she looked at me, gave me a nod and smiled. After spending time with the family, I went back upstairs and played with Shelton. He was full of energy and was wearing me out but I wasn't about to let him know that his daddy was tired. There's a funny thing about prison. It slows you down. Everything you do is controlled. You don't do anything fast. You just walk down you time...day by day, hour by hour, minute by minute. All of the excitement had me feeling a bit tired but I didn't care. Shelton and I wrestled and played with his toys until he was exhausted.

My aunt Joy finally made it over to the house. I met her outside, lifting her up off of her feet and into the evening sky. I gave her a big hug and then went walked into the house. I was realizing that my prayers were being answered. My spirit was alive and filled with a foreign kind of joy. This was a new experience for me. Sitting around, seeing everybody interact with one another, families blended, even after all that had taken place provided a peace over me. Crystal took me by my hand and led me upstairs. In her room, we took off each other's clothes and kissed. We found our way to the bed and made love. We used every inch of the bed. The sex was exciting to the both of us. We were drunk in ecstasy and then out of nowhere, her cell phone started ringing. This fucked the mood up for a hot-second. I stopped making love, looked at Crystal, and then stopped her phone from ringing. Like clockwork, she began grinding back and forth and in no time, my dick was hard again and Crystal was moaning in gratification. Her pussy was wet with passion. I could feel the wet sheets and then panting heavily, Crystal said, "Polo, I'm coming!" Hearing those words, I gripped her ass and pounded my dick inside of her at a perfect angle. "I want a little girl…you going to give me a little girl?" I said and then I nutted all inside of her.

My Job

The staff at Marshall Fall was beginning to give me a hard time. It seemed as if they were determined to send me back to prison for the remaining four to five months of my sentence. I had numerous employment opportunities that looked promising; however, none of those opportunities came to pass. Frustrated, I got a job at Kroger's with my homeboy Hillary, who was also a resident at Marshall Fall. Hillary and I had both been in Amiss State Prison together and rode the bus together to Marshall Fall when we were transferred. We started on the same day as a produce clerks and we took the job for a couple of reasons. Number one, it was not close to the center and number two, because we were allowed up to three hours to get to work and three hours to return to the center after we had gotten off. The created a huge window of opportunity to do other things with those six hours. I would work two hours out of the day and the rest of the time I would bullshit around the store and have my friends come up there to kick it with me. My supervisor had spoken to me saying, "I know why you took this job. You're only here because you living in the halfway house. Do me a huge favor and at least pretend like you like your job and make sure to speak the customers when they're within five feet of you." One particular day, Hillary and I got off at the same time and that meant that we had to return to the center together, at the same time. And if we didn't, we were going to get a lot of questions as to the reason why. If one of us fucked up, we were both in trouble. Hillary told his wife to pick him up from the Varsity downtown and I told Crystal to do the same. Crystal and I had discussed breaking the new, blue 2005 Blazer in, so when she came and picked me up, we got in the back seat and she sat on my hard dick.

A couple of days later I got back in the drug game. This was on a small-time level though. I sold ecstasy pills to a couple of people that worked with me just so I could keep some extra money in my pocket, plus I been giving Crystal bits and pieces of money because she had enrolled in medical school.

One day I called Akie and told him to come pick me up from work. When he got there, his wife Tosha was in the car with him. The three of us drove to Mike's house over in Marietta. I could tell that Mike has gotten bigger and his physique looked as if he was taking anabolic steroids. We were working out on a regular basis before I got locked up and I could tell that he was still in the gym faithfully. This is the first time that we had all been together in four years and Akie and Mike still thought that they could overpower me. They rushed me; testing my strength and I promptly threw both of them off of me before they pushed me into the wall which left a hole in it. "Got-damn nigga! Look what the fuck you did," yelled Mike. "That goes to teach y'all motherfuckers that ya'll can't fuck with me," I said. "Nigga we were just playing with your light weight ass," Akie chimed in. Tosha sat on the couch and listened to me speak about how Akie and Mike had done me when I waiting to go to trial. They both tried to explain their side of the story, but I changed the subject. We left Mike's place and rolled over to Franklin Road to see one of my other homeboy's name Snoop. Being on Franklin Road brought back a lot of memories. This is the area where we had all started off at. We were the only nigga's out here selling dope. We were the ones making all the money on Franklin Road back in the day. It felt like a reunion once we got up in Snoop's house and that made me feel good.

Back at the center, this nigga named Eric said to me, "I see you doing yo' thang. Be careful, 'cause the staff is watchin' yo ass." The following day, I left the center riding on the bus. I sat next a woman from the halfway house across the street from us and she said, "You know you're topic of discussion over at the halfway house. Every bitch in there is talking about you."

"Yeah, I heard that," I replied.

"The girls got a bet going on about who's going to be the first one to fuck you or suck your dick," she reported.

I got off at my stop and continued on my way to work. My aunt Joy came to pick me up from work when I got off. She took me back to her condo that she had just purchased. Later on in the week, my cousin, Kat had flown in town so I met my aunt at Cumberland Mall and we headed over to her house. As soon as I walked in, Kat came running out and screaming. I was so glad to see my cousin. We caught up on life and before I knew it, it was time for me to head back to Marshall Fall. My aunt Joy dropped me off but before I got out of the car, Kat told me to call Juan, her ex-boyfriend. He had given me his number since I had been in the halfway house but I hadn't gotten around to calling him just yet. Juan was my nigga. He and Kat had dated pretty strong at one time and he and I used to rob nigga's together in Atlanta and we both sold dope on Cascade Road. After his cousin Kim snitched on us to the Marietta police in 98' about a robbery that were supposed to do, we really hadn't spoken that much…but he was *still* my nigga.

Strong Minded

I called the DMV to check on the status of my driver's license and was told that all I needed to do was come in and renew it. The following day, Patrick took me the DMV downtown and within 10 minutes, I once again had a valid driver's license. After securing my license, I jumped on the bus headed to Marietta to get a haircut. I walked into Platinum Cuts and was greeted with daps and handshakes. "What's good Polo...glad you're home," my barber Ralie said. I sat down in the chair and as Ralie cut my hair, he brought me up to speed about all that had gone on will I was incarcerated. When I was done, I called Mike and asked him to come and pick me up. We went back to his apartment and chilled out for a little while. A couple of hours later, I was back at the center.

"Polo, can come in here for a second," the sergeant asked. I walked into her office and sat down in the chair facing her. "Why do you seem so depressed? You're going to be released soon and you'll be home with your family," she said. I shot her a bunch of bullshit and before long we were talking about relationships. I told her that she couldn't handle a nigga like me. She looked at me with a crazy look on her face and said in a high-pitched voice, "Why not?" I couldn't help but smirk. "Because I'm a handful. I'll drive a woman crazy, so for a woman to fuck with me, she got to be a strong minded-ass woman. I don't fuck with weak bitches," I explained. The sergeant rolled her eyes, lowered her head and looked me straight in the eyes, "So what the hell you trying to say? I'm not strong minded?" she asked with a hint of an attitude. "Nawl I'm not saying that at all. What I'm saying is that you couldn't handle me and all my shit," I replied, smiling. "You know your right, I couldn't. I'd end up killing your ass. I do know one thing about your wife Crystal. I know she's strong because you done put that girl through hell and she still by you side," she said and then continued, "even though you was fuckin' up, you must've also been doing something right because she still loves you."

Back to This Shit

How did it come back to this? Out of all the conversations that Crystal and I had, she had repeated told me that she was not ready to be a wife to me again. She had been dealing with the emotional stress and side effects from cervical cancer treatment and taking various medications. Due to her ailing health and stressed out from school, she had fallen into a state of depression. She told me that she had to deal with her personal life before she could consider being a family again. As always, I offered my help and tried to support her to the best of my ability but Crystal refused my helping hand.

We sat and talked in the visitation room at Jimmy Helms and Crystal expressed everything that she was feeling and going through mentality and emotionally and she began to cry. I held her tight in my arms and from the way that she grabbed hold of me; I could tell that she was breaking down and ready to give up. I felt like a ship out at sea being tossed back and forth between gusts of winds and waves. I called Crystal's mother, Brianna after Crystal had left. Brianna explained to me that she had seen a change in Crystal. It appeared that Crystal seemed to be digressing instead of progressing. "Crystal told me about the women's number that she found in your phone Polo," Gloria told me. Crystal was having a hard time believing that I had changed in the four-plus years that I had been in prison. "She still hasn't been able to find it in her hear to forgive you Polo. Stay strong and keep doing the right things and just continue to be there for Crystal," she encouraged me. I had always been there for Crystal, through it all. I decided to put my own issues to the side so that I could focus on taking care of Crystal and tending to my family.

Crystal told me that she could not be there for me in the same way that I was there for her. Gradually and very subtly, Crystal began to push me out of her life. She would find the most minute thing to argue about and she made mention that I was calling her too much. She no longer felt that we needed to speak to one another every day, she explained to me. "What the fuck is going on," I thought to myself. I've never been stupid. I knew the game that Crystal was playing and while I understood that she was dealing with a lot shit and tried to be there for her, I knew that she wanted me to be the one to say, "Fuck this!" and give up on our relationship.

I called Crystal on the morning of Shelton's 5th birthday and asked her if she could come and pick me up from work early so that I could come to the birthday party that she had planned for later on that day. "No, because I don't want to have to rush to get you pack to center." She said that it really didn't matter if came to the party or not because I was not being released on Shelton's anyway. Crystal was really bullshitting now I thought to myself. Those were the lamest ass excuses that I had ever heard. I felt like she was trying to play me like a chump…and I ain't nobody's chump! I had a figure out a Plan B quick. I hung up from Crystal and called my aunt Joy and asked her if she could pick me up from work and she said, "Yes Polo, that's not a problem." I thought about the conversation that Crystal and I had the rest of the day. I couldn't seem to get it out of my mind. I got off work at 3pm and I had to be back at the center by 6pm. I spoke to my supervisor and explained to him that it was my son's birthday and that I wanted to attend his birthday party. I asked him if he would be willing to fax over a letter that stated that I had to work overtime and that I would be getting off of work at 5pm instead of 3pm. I he agreed to my request, I would not have to be back at the center until 8pm instead of 6 o'clock. "I don't mind doing that at all Polo," he said and he faxed over the letter that stated as much. Aunt Joy picked me up from work as planned right at 3 o'clock. We stopped at Pets Mart so that I could buy Shelton's birthday present. I settled on a parakeet because I wanted my son to be free throughout his life and birds always represented that freedom to me. I wanted to show him that he could go anywhere and do anything in life that he so desired. I thought back my days in prison; being out in the yard and hearing birds singing and they would fly over me. Many times I wished I was one of them so that I could I fly out of the hell that I was living in.

Crystal had Shelton's party at this warehouse-type of building that was full of slides, jumps and obstacles courses. There were kids running around everywhere; yelling, laughing, jumping, playing, crying and some were even eating. It looked like a heaven for kids! Crystal looked at me with cold emptiness. I didn't seem like there was any love for me in Crystal anymore. Shelton looked up and saw me and ran over to me screaming, "Daddy, daddy!" I picked him up and hugged and kissed him. I thought back to the visits that I would receive from Crystal and Shelton when I was in prison and it didn't seem like all that much had changed, except for the fact that I was no longer incarcerated. Aside from that, our relationship was still fucked up and we weren't living as a family. Shelton had the most inquisitive look on his face as he looked at his gift that was in a box from Pets Mart so I asked him if he wanted to look inside. I opened the box halfway to tease him just a bit and his eyes opened so wide with excitement. I let him open the box all the way and he jumped back in my arms again and ran off telling anybody that would listen, "My Daddy got me a bird!" I was elated. I had not felt that good in a long, long time. I watched Shelton play for quite some time; however, Crystal still hadn't said a word to me. Was she mad that I came to my own son's party? Was she embarrassed that I was there? I couldn't help but think these things but I finally said to myself, "Fuck that! I'm here!" Whatever the problem was, I did not give a fuck! This was Shelton's first birthday that I could attend since he had been born and I would be damned if any type of bullshit was going to put me in a fucked up mood. After 30 minutes or so, Crystal walked over to me and said, "Hey." I stared her straight in her eyes with a look that let her know how heated that I was. Instead of showing my anger and causing a scene, I bit my tongue and said jokingly, "Damn, it too yo' ass long enough!"

"Polo I was talking to our guest," she responded. "Bullshit Crystal, when I first came in here, you weren't doing shit! You looked like you seen a fuckin' ghost when you saw me."

"Well, I'm sorry Polo, I'm doing a hundred things at once, and I wasn't trying to ignore you," Crystal said, visibly irritated. Everybody gathered around and sang *Happy Birthday* to Shelton. 8pm was fast-approaching so Aunt Joy and I left and headed towards the Martin Luther King Marta station. I kissed my aunt before I got out of the car and waited on my train. As soon as I arrived at Jimmy Helms, an officer asked me where I had been. I explained to him that I had to work two hours of overtime and that my supervisor had faxed over a letter that stated exactly that. He told me that they had received the fax. When I heard that, I said, "Then why the hell is y'all asking me where I been!" The officer told me that the fax wasn't real. "You signed your supervisor's name," the officer said. I was ready to explode but I maintained my composure and blew the entire exchange off. The staff let me know that they were going to make sure that I was adhering to the rules of the transition center. They couldn't prove anything; even though I had made sure to cover my ass by having my supervisor fax the letter to begin with. Unable to prove me guilty of any wrongdoing, they excused the entire "so-called" incident but let me know that they were watching me.

Turned Against Me

I tried everything to tolerate Crystal's shit and lately she had been sick, on bed rest but I did not actually know why. I would later find out that Crystal had been abusing prescriptions drugs. I was going through it at the center. I had been their main target as of late and I was ready to go off on all of their asses. I recalled how the sergeant had told me that entire staff disliked me and that they had all intentions on violating me so that they could send my black ass back to prison.

On my way to work one morning, I got off the bus and stopped by a pay phone to call a couple folks that I knew would come and pick me up. Of all the people that I called, Mike was the person that came through for me. Something in my spirit kept telling me to go to work and back to the center but for some reason; I ignored my spirit, hopped back on the bus and met Mike out in Cumberland Mall, where he picked me up. We stopped and got something to eat at Applebee's and then we rode over to the pet store because I needed to buy some mice to feed to my Red Tail Boa Constrictor that Mike had been taking care of for me. Back at Mike's apartment, I fed my snake and he and I talked about what was going on in the streets; about who was fuckin' with who, which nigga's had the work, dope prices and everything else under the sun. Everything was seemed to be going good that morning until Mike informed me that he was not going to be able to take me to work. I thought I had heard him wrong. "What the fuck you mean you can't take me to work?" I asked Mike. "Look, Polo I ain't got time to take you," Mike responded. "Nigga it ain't gone take you no time to drop me off at work nigga," I said seething. "Polo, if I take you to work I'm gone miss out on too much money dog," Mike explained. "Money? Mothafucka, you putting money over me...you want me to get back on the bus to get to work? That shit will take two hours and if you take me, it'll take 20 minutes!" I ranted. "Polo I can't do it," he said and with that, our conversation was over. He drove me back to Cumberland Mall but I got of the car, I told him, "I'm gone end up back in prison because of this hoe shit, cause I'm gone be 2-3 hours late to work and they gone call the center talking 'bout I ain't showed up for work!"

"So what if you do," Mike interrupted, "you only got a couple months until you max out for good anyway." I looked at Mike like he was a complete stranger and said, "Fuck you!" and got out of his car.

I called my supervisor and notified him that I was going to be late and he told me that it wasn't a problem but to hurry up and get there. I arrived to work two-and-a-half hours late. The store manager asked me why I was late and I explained to him that I had notified my supervisor that I would be tardy. "Your supervisor did not convey that information to me," the store manager said and then he told me to get to work. Thirty minutes later, I was paged to the front of the store over the intercom. As I approached the customer service desk, I saw the first shift sergeant and another officer from Marshall Fall. The sergeant told me to gather my things because we needed to go back to the center. He also informed me that I was *not* in trouble. As I walked to the back of the store, I contemplated running out the back door and escaping to freedom. There was only one thing wrong with that plan; I would end up the run for the rest of my life; therefore, I did as the officer had instructed me and gathered my belongings and headed back to Marshall Fall.

As soon as I arrived at the center, I was told to go to the superintendent's office. . While I waited on the superintendent, one of the officers served me with a disciplinary report or a "D.R." as we referred to them. The charges that were listed against me was, "Unauthorized Absence and Failure to Follow". The sergeant that I was cool with walked in and told me that she needed to speak with me immediately. We went into her office and I closed the door behind me. We both sat down and the sergeant said, "Where have you been" in a stern yet caring tone. Always one to be able to think on my feet, I quickly replied, "At work."

"Nawl, nigga where have you been?" she asked.

"What are you talking about Serge?" I inquired, playing the dumb roll. "Why in the hell were you two and a half hours late getting to work Polo?" she asked, "I know you been somewhere else."

"I haven't been anywhere other than work," I reassured the serge. "Dickson, look!" she said. "Look at what? Whatever I tell you, you not gone believe me. If you believe that I was somewhere else, then I been somewhere else, right?" I asked in a rhetorical manner. "Just tell me where you been," the Serge pleaded. I made up a story and told her that I had left my wallet on top of a pay phone at the Martin Luther King Center and that I had gone back to get it once I realized that was where I had left it. I strengthened my lie by informing her that I had called my supervisor and notified him that I would be late and that he was fine with that. "So you mean to tell me that you went back to retrieve your wallet that you left at a pay phone?" she asked as if she didn't believe my story. "What were you doing using the phone in the first place, you know it's against the rules. Mr. Dickson, I don't know what to say, your story sounds good, but I know you're lying. The superintendent wants to talk to you so wait outside while I get him on the phone. I'll call you back in here in a second," and she began dialing someone from her office phone. I left her office and went straight to the phone and called Crystal.

Crystal answered the phone. "Crystal," I said. "What's wrong Polo, why you sound like that?" Crystal asked. "Crystal listens. I might be going back to prison," I began to explain. "WHAT!" she screamed. "Listen baby, I might or I might not," I told her. The sergeant called me back into her office so I hung up the phone and went back into the Serge's office. I got on the phone with the superintendent and told him the same exact story that I had told the sergeant. He told me that he would speak to on Monday morning. I asked him if I still had my weekend pass to go home and he informed me that my privileges had been taken away until this matter was resolved. I called Crystal back but this time when she answered the phone, all she said was, "What?"

"Damn, chill the fuck out," I said. "Polo, you hung up in my face, now tells me what's going on," Crystal griped. I told her everything that had gone down and she instantly began to go off on me. I talked to the sergeant in her office all night long and she kept telling me not to worry about the D.R. and that superintendent was not going to send me back to prison. Monday rolled around and I walked to the superintendent's office. He notified me that I was being transferred to Jackson State Prison until my D.R. had been investigated.

Back in Chains

Once again shackled from head to toe, I rode in the van on my way to my transfer to Jackson. Walking into the prison grounds, I gazed around at this building that I had prayed that I would never have to see again; the razor-wire fence, the guard tower that rested in each corner of the prison that was occupied by at least one correctional officer armed with a mini-fourteen rifle and the inmates that milled about. Jackson State Prison was a close-security prison and by now it had become the prison where condemned prisoners were executed. In the days when death row inmates were put to death by the electric chair, all executions were done at one of Georgia's most dangerous prison's, Georgia State Prison, better known as Reidsville. Georgia had not used the electric chair since June 10, 1998, when David Loomis Cargill was put to death. The legal and preferred method executed condemned men and women in the state of Georgia now was lethal injection, due to the fact that the electric chair method had been deemed "cruel and unusual". Back inside of Jackson, I was ordered to strip naked, spread my ass-cheeks apart, lift my nuts up and squat and cough, all while an officer inspected me, assuring that that I did not possess any kind of contraband. How could a man enjoy a job like this; telling another man to strip, spread his ass apart, grab his nuts, squat and cough, I thought to myself. I hated doing this shit. It was degrading. After getting dressed, I was taken to the segregation unit which was located in D-building and placed in cell fifty. There were sounds of yelling, cats screaming at one another and I could not help but smell the indescribable stench of prison. The iron-clad bars made a vibrated sounded that bounced off the cinder-block prison walls reminiscent of thunder when they would open and close. I sat in my cell and thought about Crystal and Shelton and about how I had fucked up once again. There was a wild madness running around in my mind and I felt like killing myself. I began to daydream about all of the things that I would do when I was finally released from prison like, taking vacations, enjoying the holidays, having family dinners. The one thing that I could not help but constantly think of was how I was going to make money upon my release. I wanted to put my hands into every pot of gold that I possibly could. As my mind drifted, I once-again realized the blessings that God had bestowed upon me up until this point. I also gained a better perspective and understanding of what Crystal had told me, "Polo, I'm not ready to be a wife and a family again." I had spent 33 days in the hole as I waited for my case involving my disciplinary report. I had been found guilty of both charges which meant that the remaining 4 or 5 months would be served on the inside of one of Georgia's state prisons. My 33rd night at Jackson proved to be my last one there. I was transferred to Wayne State Prison the following morning.

Wayne State was a fucked up prison. It was a completely protective custody prison. This is where the Department of Corrections would send all the lawyers, doctors, police, judges and high profile inmates that had been convicted and sentenced to prison. This is also where some regular inmates that feared for their lives were sent if and when the department of corrections had substantial evidence to determine that those particular inmates did indeed require protective custody. I saw a guy that I recognized instantly. He was an ex-police officer that had been a member of the Red Dog unit which provided aggressive policing in neighborhoods that had high rates of dope dealing and crimes to the use and sale of drugs. I came to find out that he had been convicted of robbing dope dealers and sentenced to prison for his offenses. There was another man that I recognized as well. He was also an ex-police officer that was convicted and sentence to life for the rape of several women. It seems as though he would pull them over for supposed traffic violations, place them into custody and then proceed to rape them. The most interesting guy that I recognized was Ray Brent Marsh. I remembered seeing his story all over the news for months. The police had raided his Tri-State Crematory in Walker county Georgia and discovered dead bodies all over the place that had not been cremated. He was arrested on over 300 criminal violations, charged with over 700 counts and convicted of theft by deception, abusing a corpse, burial service related fraud and giving false statements. He eventually copped a plea and was serving 12 years. I also saw the karate instructor who had molested the children that he taught. The list went on and on.

Eleven days had passed since I first arrived at Wayne State Prison and it was eight days before my tentative release date. I was still in a state of depression and I hadn't heard anything from the find myself still in a state of mind of depression, I haven't heard nothing from the Georgia State Board of Pardons and Paroles; the people that would ultimately decide when I would be released from custody. I didn't know if I would going home on May 2, 2006, as had been the case before I was sent back from Jimmy Helms or if I would be forced to serve out remainder of my entire five-year term. Wayne State was super-boring. There wasn't any gambling, any drugs, and no happenings. Nothing was happening which meant that there was nothing to do...except time. I referred to this prison as the retirement home. Wayne State was also full of snitches. They told on everything that a nigga did! Most of these motherfuckers couldn't survive anywhere else. Within 30 days, most of them would have been dead if they would have been serving time at another prison. The closes thing to a fight that I had had so far was an argument; nothing else, nothing more. I didn't have anything else to do, so I started scaring the cowards up in there. I would talk shit to them all day long. If I would have been serving long time in Wayne State, I would have been slapping around a good number of the bitch-ass nigga's that were in there.

My anticipate release date had passed and a week letter I received a letter from the board that notifying me that would not be released until my original max out date which as August 22, 2006. Reading the letter I was like fuck it. I only had three more months to do. I pulled out a sheet of paper and began writing a poem. It went something like this:

Still these folks won't let me go, sending me a paper of what the chairman wrote.

"We decided to extend your parole month to max" clearly to state the facts

The time I lost I will never get back

Now I'm about to explode, my x-wife turning up her nose because I'm supposed to be home putting my hands in pots of gold.

Five voted against me taking away my parole date, as I pick away this pain out my brain, I claim peace, but reality the game they play will have all their children in a place screaming out of rage, scared to touch the flames from the chain

And will never know the reason why we call this shit a gang

The prison system is overcrowded, instead of you releasing me, for these last three months, you want to house me

Now tell me what you think I'll do if I see you on the streets, will you start shaking in your jeans, apologizing for not releasing me.

Now your family can't sleep, their heart skips a beat every time the news comes on "body found" you have been missing for several weeks.

You don't understand its consequences when you fuck with some-one's freedom, fire coming out of my heater taking you away from your people.

I went to the yard to get some air and ended up talking to Ray, Ray Brent Marsh from Tri-State Crematory. He explained to me how he had gotten caught up with all those bodies and why he had not cremated them even though he had been paid to do so. Basically he said that people didn't know where the ashes that he gave them came from. He'd burn wood and give those ashes to a grieving fam-ily and they never knew that what they actually had was wood ashes and not those of their loved-one. We talked for a little while and then I went back inside the dorm. Each day I prayed to God, that He would mold me into the man that I was meant to be. The road that I had been on had been a very difficult one. I had been away from my family for almost 5 years but prison had not changed me; however, it did provide me with a greater appreciation for the things that I valued most in life – which were my freedom, Crystal and Shelton. My incarceration had revealed all that God had blessed me with. I appreciated the little shit in my life now. Things like walking to the mailbox, answering my own phone or being able to rest in my own tub and take a nice hot bath. I never wanted to go down this road again. I had lost so much along this journey. On the early, dew-ridden morning of August 22, 2006, I walked out of the Georgia Department of Corrections prison system; a free man. I had made it out in one piece. I went in as a man and I came out a better man. I gained a tremendous amount of mental strength from being behind the walls of various institutions. The sun was peeking out of the hazy sky as I walked toward the parking lot. Standing off in the distance I could see my aunty Joy. There she stood arms wide open, smiling from ear-to-ear. She had always been a saving grace-type of element in my life and here she was, once again to help me along in my walk of life. I had a new lease on life. I thought about everything that had led me to this point: Fort Wayne, Indiana, Houston, Texas, Georgia, all the crimes, the dope I had sold, the women that I had been with. I had a checkered past to say the least. I'd had some setbacks and I had paid the price for the decisions that I had made. I vowed to be a better man this time around and closed the book on my prison experience. It had been another piece to the puzzle of my life and as I rode back to Atlanta with my aunt Joy, looking out the window under the early morning sun, I saw my life in its entirety. I accepted my shortcomings and promised myself and God that I would continue to grow and add new pieces to my puzzle; positive pieces. This is my life. This is my story. And now maybe you can see the cracks in my perfect picture.

The End